deep dark light

'Do not imagine that,
if something is hard for you to achieve,
it is therefore impossible for any man: but rather
consider anything that is humanly possible and
appropriate to lie within your own reach too.'

- Marcus Aurelius (121–180)

by
Mark Sheeky

Pentangel Books

Deep Dark Light written by Mark Sheeky.
Illustrations and graphic design by Mark Sheeky.

1st edition, published in Great Britain by Pentangel Books.
www.pentangel.co.uk

ISBN 978-0-9571947-4-8

Printed and bound by Amazon Createspace.

To Deborah, my love and light.

CONTENTS

DREAM JOURNEY INTO MARK SHEEKY'S DEEP DARK LIGHT

By Kenneth Pobo

Probably a good place to start thinking about this work is the title. Usually these words are separate, like individual ships on the water. Not here. It's not that these three entities don't exist—but sometimes in one is the other. He could have begun with Dark or Light, but he chose Deep—and that's where we're headed, a deep place, a steep place full of questions, things that form and unform at the same moment.

If you are looking for a straight-up narrative work, move along. Connections happen here—in each illustration and written piece—but these are not built from traditional forms of narrative. The words converse with the illustrations. Sometimes we clearly overhear what they say; other times we have to go strictly by impulse and intuition. In John Lennon's song "Intuition" the speaker says that intuition takes him everywhere. Everywhere, nowhere, light, dark.

Sheeky says "Our life. This shape is unique to us..." and like the illustrations that sometimes resemble Rorschach ink blots we look for meaning, for depth, in those shapes. It isn't the poet or illustrator's job to create that meaning. We have work to do. We have to take the journey to find the meaning—with no guarantees that we will find it.

i

We might be able to find it speaking to us in a dream. Poe said that all that we see or seem is but a dream within a dream: deepdarklight. Perhaps even more than the written words, the illustrations evoke a sense of being in a dreamscape. The words feel like shapes, perhaps incandescent figures our beings, as we enter the surprise of imagery that forms only to bust apart.

Time. Is it another dream? We mark our way with time. It's like a cane everybody walks with. It's also a way to create meaning out of our days. "Everything is all about escapism," says Sheeky's speaker. We want to escape time. We want time to be kind to us, to remember us. Time is busy passing. It can't look back even as we scream out.

Also present are creators from earlier times. They feel as real here as we do. Their words aren't monuments unless monuments have dreams, which maybe they do. "The sky explodes infinitely." We observe and partake of it. Great creators of the past are part of that ongoing explosion. That might sound lovely, but we are reminded too that "Existence is war." The exploding sky mimics war and war mimics the exploding sky as dark and light tangle with each other.

Meet George. He's assembling a sculpture. He's a maker. He is caught/free from being caught between dusk and dawn. In a tenuous world, he makes. Winter. Spring. Winterspring. Dreamgeorge—he "steps into the delightful coolness." Yet loss comes near. Where is Lucine? Time ages too. "Love is a blindfold chosen deliberately." We could choose to see. We may prefer not to see.

Birds. They appear and fly away before we can really see them well. They're dreams. Perhaps they are moments that take shape–take flight–we remember them and wait for them to return. Without warning an ape appears. We must face it. The path feels like it fades as we go down it. The stone clock is dead, yet we feel time. Childhood comes up to us in our present life, maybe more real than our present life.

A sound of bells. "George, the leaf in the brook, float-ing in the sunlit water." Transience. Trying to find meaning, trying to find people, when they disappear. The last poem, "Light," reminds us of Ozymandias. The speaker asks him to "loosen every dream." And the last two words are "bright sky." Has darkness been van-quished or lessened? Or is the ending not an ending at all–but a moment, a bright sky that appears now but will not last.

THE CAVERN OF DOORS

The great bronze gates,
towering elephants on needle pin feet,
so heavy, we push.
A vast chamber beyond, circular,
polished stone floor,
like being inside a wedding-cake palace,
ring after ring,
doorway after doorway,
a thousand doors on each level, a million,
and level upon level, like a rope up and up to an
infinite white point

sun, sky, star...

PREFACE

This book is in three parts, like a sonata of music, and that was my aim, to create a sonata of writing, a book driven by mood and structure at least as much as narrative.

Parts touch upon philosophy and science; principally the philosophy of self, reason, and meaning. This book does not pretend to break any new intellectual ground in this regard, but as part of its mood-driven structure it engages in a quest for purpose as a precursor to the story that is the finalé.

Let us begin.

Mark Sheeky, 2018.

'In Xanadu did Kubla Khan
A stately pleasure dome decree:
Where Alph, the sacred river, ran
Through caverns measureless to man
Down to a sunless sea.'

- Samuel Taylor Coleridge (1772–1834)

deep

THE BEGINNING

The infinite-sun screams,
its hissing whiteness.

Neutrino beams flee,
leaving 'Tetris' holes.

Who did this?

Not me.

Not I.

TORTURED

My guts wriggle like a gaggle of worms in a pit,
grasping for a distant sunlight bit.

My head boils,
a rock of thought inside,
a high pressure acid lump, crying,
for help, comfort.

What hope is there?

What a loss it would be to find a gift for humanity on
an island,
alone,
unable to find even food,
and yet have the gift,
and yet no food.

What a loss it is,
to have an impotent gift.

We must scream to that island sky in mourning.

Even on an island, we
are driven by society,
by the demand to succeed
and survive, to build a future.

For the Michaelangelo of cave-painting
to focus on the cave painting, however glowing,
to the exclusion of sustenance,
is impossible.

For the Michaelangelo of cave-painting
to focus on hunting, when ineffective at hunting,
to the exclusion of cave painting,
is impossible.

I am zugzwanged.
I am star-crossed.
I am doomed.

On our last day,
what might we regret?

THE ISLAND

I step lonely over this shore, warm sand,
the scent of coconuts and no crabs,
no tea.

Nothing to eat.

My wet eyes blink at the distant clouds,
as seen by Alexander Selkirk.

Our sentiments meet.

How long life is, so long,
infinitely so, we know only life.

We know death only from its observation in others.

Others stop communicating with us:
they are dead.
Our cells stop communicating with us:
they are dead.
The most distant stars are out of sight, faster than
light.
The most distant stars stop communicating with us:
they are dead.
This knife carves our universe into its present form,
and this shape is called life.

Our life. This shape is unique to us, each thing, each
sector.
Each sector of the universe can send and receive
unique data,

and as this communication reflects life,
so each life is unique in form.

Two distant stars communicate:
dead to us, but alive to each other.
Does this prove life beyond death?

Life is the communication of information.

I touch the gritty sand,
and raise a sunken shell to my ear.
The shell communicates a wistful moan,
a sunless sigh.

I whisper to this new friend,
a greeting to Alexander Selkirk.
I sense his soul reply,
here in nothing,
on a beach of nowhere,
with only you, the reader
of these tragic words.

I cast the shell into the sea.

I step lonely over this shore, warm sand,
the scent of coconuts and no crabs,
no tea.

Nothing to eat.

How long life is, so long,
infinitely so, we know only life.

THE INEFFECTUAL HUNTER

To an artist, starvation is the best death.
Anything less is selling out.

Let the form of his last breath be a beautiful curl,
a best, last gift for a cold, blind, world.
Let the dance of his falling corpse evoke a lost
moment.
Let his sculpture of bones be an inspirational
monument.
Let his uncleaned dish signify pity.
Let his works endure, and give comfort by empathy.

An artist is loved indirectly.

HOW GREAT THOU ART

As a lonely cloud, when I in awesome wonder...

The greatest artists are dead, it seems.
We see their work in mausoleums and museums, and
we love them.

We consider all the works their hands have made...

It is easy to attach love to the dead,
they are no threat, and can't spring surprises.
We can collect them, like favourite flavours of ice-
cream,
without affiliation or social risk.

I see the stars...

Even dead dictators who painted,
can have their paintings appreciated,
irrespective of their political legacy,
or alleged-carpet-chewing antics (you know who you
are).

I hear the rolling thunder...

Most artworks result from personal skills,
developed for solitary reasons without apparent social
value,
and are regarded suspiciously,
for the world values utility.

Thy power throughout the universe displayed...

The living can hide their wealth, their love, their
genius, their knowledge, their connections, their
personal skills developed for solitary reasons.
The dead reveal everything.

We compete with the living.
We have defeated the dead.

And yet, we can be touched by those
who create small things that reflect our souls.
This conveyance of information is the energy of life.

Then sings my soul, how great thou art.

TIME

The present is the border between the past and
future,
slicing time into day and night like a planet's
terminator,
sharpest where perception is fastest,
more blunt where perception is slow.

The effect affects a cause as equally as a cause affects
an effect.

Time is a matter of perception.
We can perceive only the past because light moves,
and our perceptions are based upon light,
or slower media such as sounds or smells.

From the perception of a timeless being or light-ray
there is time but no past or future,
for there is no motion.

From the perception of a timeless being or light-ray
all things become a perfect-crystal-scuplture of all-
things. One eternal perfect-crystal-scuplture.

The fact that the past can be perceived,
but that the future cannot be perceived,
does not make the past more special than the future;
we are powerless to change either.

Our perceptions and understanding can corrupt our
view of the future.

Our perceptions of our environment and our deteriorating memory can corrupt our view of the past.

Truth is lost via imperfect perception.

Can perception be perfect?
Can any fragment of perception be perfect?
Can any fragment of perception of any fragment of the universe be perfect?

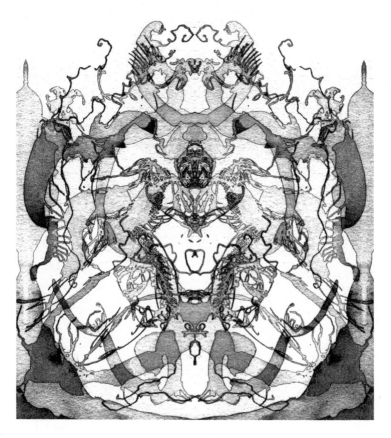

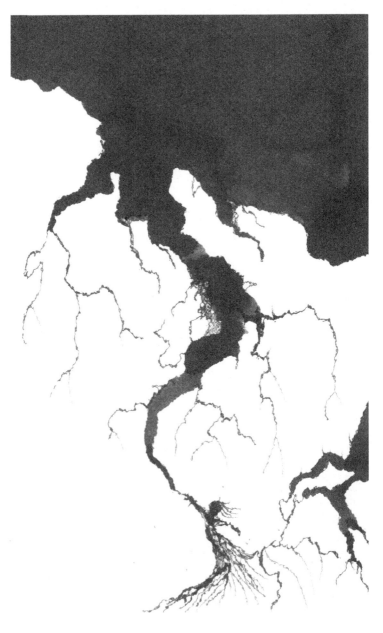

14

LIFE

Life is the communication of information;
the more we communicate, the more alive we are.

The more silence we endure, the more we kill.
Blink, and slice some imagery into oblivion,
the guillotine of sight.
Each unread word kills a fragment of an author.
Ignorance is murder.

The more doors we close, the more life we slice away
from the universe of others.
The more we shine out, the more life we give.

HOPE

Poor people are religious,
for they need hope in their lives.

Imaginative people grasp at magic when faced with
the incredulity of ancient dogma.
Pity Crowley, for he needed hope.

Philosophers are eternally restless and seek
understanding,
for they need hope in their lives.

Nihilists seek perfect love,
for they need hope, the fools,
as if a thing like that
could exist.

Idiots are happy,
one assumes,
if idiots really exist.

Are Mayflies contented?

All young things love life, which grows forever.
Pity the universe, when past half of its age.

The more adept we become at predicting the future,
the worse the feeling becomes.
The more adept we become at predicting the future,
the more we need hope.
Middle-class Buddhists talk of living in 'the now'
to escape their 'scrying'.

It is all about escapism.

Everything is all about escapism.
Everything is all about escapism.
Everything is all about escapism.

ESCAPE

Escape, where?

What is this place we can aspire to,
this heaven and control over our whirling lives?
How good could it be?

That which is unconsidered, is perfect.

We are not in control, and we can never escape,
this knowledge is the best heaven
that there can be.

LOVE

Free, with the song of angel voices,
in blue sky fresh,
and crystal waterclouds,
of sun-rays' love.

Free in love, that yellow-light chemical bliss,
of transparent restfulness,
this magical pure flow.

Freedom cannot be,
for it lives only in imagination,
but infinite communication is possible, one imagines...
except for the limits of infinity, time and space,
although some information is lost, always.

Some information is lost, in replication.
Some information can be lost, and never regained,
the inevitability of death,
of even atomic nuclei.

More love is always given than received,
and some is lost by loving that which is dead,
which amounts to lost energy.

We can give what we have to all things,
and we can receive up to our capacity from all things,
but some information is damaged or corrupted or lost,
and this trickle leads to a decline in capacity,
and the ability to communicate accurately.

Some information is lost, in replication.

Some information can be lost, and never regained,
the inevitability of death,
of even atomic nuclei.

A black sand particle in the hour-glass,
treading water.

A heaven glimpsed in a wild flower,
the dye in the petals shivering.

A teardrop falls.

IMAGINATION

What might be, causes angst.
What could be, causes angst.
What might be!
What could be!

The mind can imagine any world,
but is never satisfied with the actual world.

The mind can imagine peace when we are on fire,
and we are always dissatisfied with the fire.

The mind can imagine a heaven when we are happy
and at peace,
and we are always dissatisfied with the happiness and
the peace.

Can the mind assemble the structures of the actual
world?

How would we know?

Perhaps we can test the accuracy of our fantasies,
with our level of satisfaction?

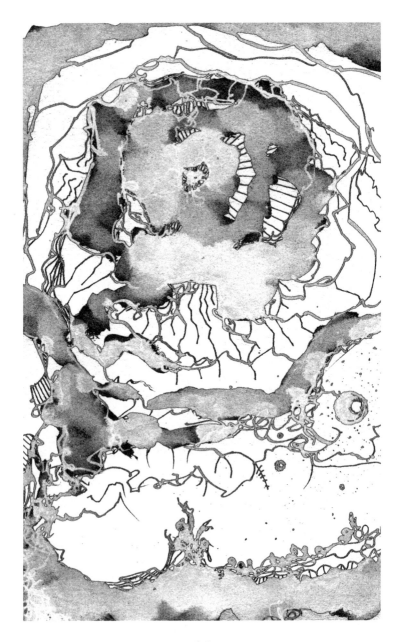

24

THE END

The black sky laments
with Mellotron-choirs of memory.

Oh how the fragments
of youth crisp away,
leaving holes in shellac webs,
for wistful recollection,
the stubby black candlewicks,
of intellect that live,
in hope of re-ignition,
but not knowing why.

Who did this?

Not me.

Not I.

'If you would be a real seeker after truth,
it is necessary that at least once in your life
you doubt, as far as possible, all things.'

- René Descartes (1596–1650)

dark

'Come here, look!' said Lucine, the spirit-girl. She took George's hand and led him though the dark trees, crisping through the pine scented branches. A clearing opened up before them and George found himself in a bright sky of cold, clear air. He was standing on the top of a cliff before a wide sea that stretched to an infinite distance.

'It is a sea of possibility,' she said, 'every thought is here, every feeling, every musical phrase, every remarkable image...'

George remained awestruck: 'But this must be as large as the entire universe..?'

'Of course,' she said, 'and you have one lifetime to touch and sip any part, from any perspective you choose. You can do this each day, for one whole lifetime.'

DARKNESS

I awake in an infinitely dark space, a vast and empty universe.

Gradually, my eyes grow accustomed to a strange, pervasive light, weak grey. I see two grey spheres.

I am afraid.

'I put you here!' speaks a devilish voice.

'Who are you??' I instantly suspected Descartes' demon.

'Welcome back...' speaks the voice.

BED

4am and wide awake
in deep dark light.
4am and burning
in deep dark night.
A black-hole soul burns,
a wide eyes gaze, to see,
no hope inside this maze,
of dead ends.

It feels all explored,
all the ends feel dead
but they are not, for
feelings are romantic.
Romantic.
Pass the laundenum overdose.

For the atheist realist,
there is no rational hope.
One's escapism must be in history's arms,
the lives of part artists
who could not see their light.
We must see ours and cling to its weak warmth,
in love,
to each day do our best,
shine our heart to the cold dark sky above.

The genius is forever alone,
in mind in soul, inside.
It is in this place, this crucible
where the heart of pi resides.

I saw the last digit of pi today,
burning at the end of time and space,
flickering a tiny hello
from a place of pure beauty.
There is a lens that makes all of its digits one.

LOVE

Dearest Lucine, I have discovered the most wonderful thing, that we are connected. Each of us lives only in the minds of others. We can know ourselves, but we cannot ever know what came before us, or what comes after us. Our lives, from our perspective, are infinite. Life, death, the passage of time, these are social constructs, things only exist in others, the people we see. We know death only through seeing it in others, and by feeling the decay in ourselves. We cannot die ourselves; we exist, then do not. How can anything experience non-existence?

We are all citadels of cells, tiny animals that work together to make us. Tiny animals, trying hard to make their own way, each sharing, loving, giving.

Our perspective of the universe is unique. This makes our experience of the universe unique, but also makes our knowledge unique, our truth unique and therefore our universe unique. There is no shared universe, we each have a personal universe, and you are in mine.

There was a time when you were alive in mine.

You exist in my memory.

DARK KNOWLEDGE

I awake in an infinitely dark space, a vast and empty universe.

Gradually, my eyes grow accustomed to a strange, pervasive light, and I see two grey spheres. I cannot hear, smell or otherwise detect anything else. I cannot move or look around. My knowledge consists of what?

I know that the universe contains two spheres. Perhaps there are other things behind me? Would my ability to look backwards add to my knowledge? If so then my field of vision is a factor, it follows that to see more creates more knowledge. It does, for I am deriving knowledge only from what I can see and have no other senses.

I awoke here, what of my life before waking? I know nothing. In this place, waking up is the same as being born, appearing spontaneously. This is an exceptionally abstract universe. The spheres probably feel the same way I do.

I go blind. What do I know about the universe now? I might think that there are two spheres, but that is merely my memory.

XANADU

The crystal castle of the mind
a temple of experience,
where fingertips of reason find
conclusions, each unverified,
beneath an inside sky.

Truth is personal because any facts will always out-
number the amount of resources to analyse them,
leaving an element of interpretation to every situation.
Although a changing fact might change a conclusion,
there will always be several possibilities of truth that
match the observable data, so each option is equally
true at the same time.

There can be no pure truth, no right answers, just
opinions with degrees of rightness and wrongness,
and what measures right and wrong? Nobody except
our personal judgement.

'Everything is right,' speaks the demon.

'Yet even that is your opinion.'

Descartes' dogs are alive, and feel. Is that not true? If
truth is consensus then it depends upon communication. How can an atom or moon express its thoughts
and feelings? We must try to interpret them, it is the
only fair way.

LOVE

Dearest Lucine, I can feel you when you are far away, know your thoughts and know that you are thinking of me. Love is this common flow. Our cells are as one, as mine are to form my body, as yours are to form yours. If we isolated them, could we see them as separate entities? The similarities between them would far out-weigh their differences. Are we one being, or two?

When you are with me, how close are you? When you are not, how close are you?

These golden threads of energy are lines of powerful understanding, commonality. We become one, larger being than each of us alone. That is the power we have.

40

DARK THOUGHT

I am born blind in an infinitely dark space, a vast and empty universe, with no previous knowledge, and no other senses. What do I know?

I know that I think, and nothing more, but when I think, what is happening? What I consider to be consciousness is an observation of my thoughts, a sense that detects the flow of information inside me. A sense as valid and tangible, as flawed and subject to distortions, as sight. Can I think without observing my thoughts? No. What I know as thought is the observation of internal information, that's what the word means. That's what the word 'thought' means to me, to us.

Now you, reader, and I, are a couple. Language and its meaning depends on mutual accord between more than one person. To the only being in the universe, the word 'thought' means nothing, and so the only being in the universe cannot think.

With you, reader, and I, knowledge has already expanded a dimension to become based on an accord of language, rather than be an absolute fact, and all this despite the fact that here I am, in an infinitely dark space, supposedly alone. In this simplest of scenarios, there is complexity.

An uncommunicated fact does not exist. Who could say it did?

George swam in the warm water, selected shapes at will, like molecule models, sculptures of interest and delight.

He rested on the beach beneath a warm white sun. With an infinite sea, which is correct to keep?

'Anything,' said Lucine, 'anything that you like. That's the criteria. There is a path that flows in the universe that draws shapes, shapes that twist and curl, carving curves. The path flows through everything, it's tendrils extends from start to finish, from an exploding spider of white-light spines, into an infinite sea. You, George, are one of those paths, as am I...'

She looked up at the sun. A small bird, a tiny flake circled it in a joyous sweeping motion.

George looked upon the collection of objects that he had assembled on the beach, the many sculptures. A feeling of deja-vu flashed through him.

43

DARK SENSE DATA

I am born blind and with no senses.

I think. Thought is the observation of the flow of internal information. The origin of this internal information either comes from external senses, or is inherent. Is there any inherent information inside me apart from sense data? How would I know?

No memory or piece of information could exist unchanging forever, if so it could not have come into being. If it was always there, then its existence is relative to what?

If information can appear inside us by growth or acquisition, then a sense must have put it there. That's what the word sense means. If something put it there, that thing would be, by definition, a sense, therefore all of the information inside us is sense data.

'Wait!' said the demon. 'That doesn't prove that all of the information inside us originates from our senses, just that if any does, you reserve the right to create a sense as its source.'

If there is information inside us, then we must be able to detect it, use it, tell someone about it. If we can't, then it's the same as not having any information. If we can, then it can be sensed by our minds at least, and whether it had a sensory origin or not, the act of communicating it means that it can be detected by a sense of the recipient.

MOTHS

Somewhere in a cyan sky, in a clear heaven-air of young sun, flew a tiny, dark bird. It was a swift, and the same age as George, the man far, far down in the sea below.

The bird snapped at a tiny moth, a morsel of food. The moth was two days old, although it had spent a few months as a caterpillar. As a caterpillar it spent a lot of time eating. It ate leaves almost every waking minute, always afraid of the shadows that flickered past over-head. It loved the taste of leaves. It didn't think of the plant as a living thing.

The bird's first thought and experience was being in a nest, being hungry, making a noise, and being fed. It hatched from an egg, but its mother couldn't tell it such a thing, or its father or siblings. It couldn't remember the egg either, it was too young.

At some point, the bird realised that it was alive. It didn't think that the moth was alive, though. If the moth was alive, it was tough luck for the moth. The bird was hungry.

DARK THOUGHT

I think. Thought is being aware of the movement of information inside me. This requires a store of inform- ation, a pathway for the information to move along, a sense to detect this, and time. Movement requires time and space.

If the storage of sense data, my memories, are changed without my awareness, can this be thought too, an unconscious thought?

All data corrupts over time. When storing any inform- ation it can either remain the same, or be changed, and when changed it becomes inaccurate. Any process that can change information has a possibility of cor- rupting or destroying part of it. Corrupt or erroneous information can't accidentally become accurate, because accidents are caused by random chance, and are ignorant. If there is any possibility to change or update information, corruption of the information, therefore, becomes inevitable, and the number of errors will increase over time.

What is it about time that corrupts? Information is sent, information is received. Can it be changed between being sent and received? If it cannot, then how could information be acquired at all, for it would always remain a pure, unadulterated copy. Two identical pieces of information are the same as one piece in every way, that's what identical means. Information requires manipulation to be processed and used.

If information can be changed between being sent and received, then it is inevitable that some quantity, however tiny, is lost or corrupted. Sending information requires motion, which requires time and space. It is reasonable to assume that information loss can occur across both equally.

If my memories can be stored, then errors in my memory are inevitable.

What then of the unconscious thought? Can my memory be changed without my awareness?

When thinking, I might notice a change in my memory. I could only notice if I had a separate copy, a reference copy, to detect the change. I might notice that my memory does not correspond to reality. Perhaps reality has changed, perhaps my memory has changed. It is impossible to say which without another reference copy, another being, another sense.

REQUIEM FOR A MILLION CELLS

I drift in crowds.
I glimpse the dark echo of my face in a window.
It looks old.
I am old.
How did this happen?

Cells fragment.
They hold aloft loved structures,
this dusty cathedral,
monument to our every experience.

This web of tiny animals,
our always-friends
who live and die for us,
yet never know us.

We are composite beings. All things are composites
because reality and truth are dependent upon sharing
information and observation. We create reality by
accepting information because information can only
be proven to exist when transmitted and absorbed.

We send a super-thin light ray as a signal into dark
distant space. It contains a secret message. If the message is never intercepted, does it exist? Not if we, the
sender, also forget about it because the universe
would operate in every way identically to a universe
without the light ray. If it operated differently (as perhaps if someone notices the missing energy) then the
ray would instantly exist.

LET THERE BE LIGHT

I awake with my eyes closed, with no other senses or prior memories. Light does not exist.

I open my eyes, and see some light. Light exists.

Does this mean that energy has been spontaneously created by my eyes?

Yes. It took light and eyes to create it. Light without eyes, or eyes without light would not be sufficient.

Can we prove that light was there before I opened my eyes? No, light was not there, nor energy. To detect either would create it.

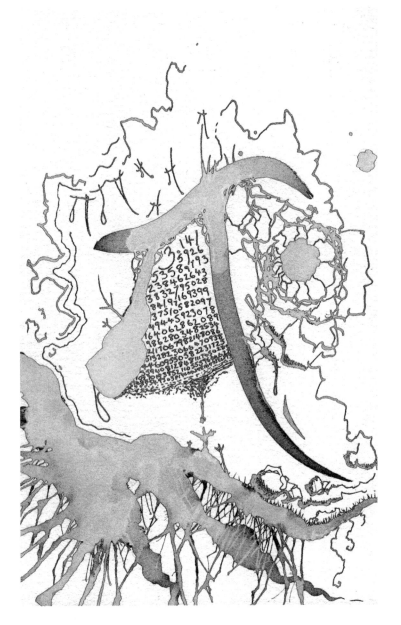

50

PERFECTION

Pi, in unreachable heaven.
To stroke its number-line,
the ever receding filaments of perfection.

Filaments of crystal, diamond, adamant. Impervious.

You cannot change perfection, or experience it. It exists only theoretically, like a perfect sphere, like a perfect circle, like a perfect curve, like a perfectly straight line. Just as a straight line is a curve in curved space, even in straight space, a line, a track, cannot exist as a pure form in reality. Reality is essentially imperfect because perfection is infinitely pervasive.

Reality can squish as closely as it can towards a mathematical perfection, but can never attain it.

The sky explodes infinitely. Everywhere is engulfed by black spines.

BLACK HOLE

Falling towards perfection.

We approach a black hole. Nothing can escape, not light or information. If nothing can escape, then nothing can enter, or else something would be lost from the universe, and loss is forever, infinite.

Here it hums. There is nothing beyond the event horizon, it is a wall, a border, an edge that can never be breached. This edge is the edge of the universe.

Everything lives just outside of the perimeter, pushed there when this bubble formed. Its dimensions are formed and dependant only on the substances at its perimeter.

A hollow sphere, of sorts, with an infinitely impenetrable heart, not infinite in character for it is defined by the life at its perimeter. It is a convex edge.

It cannot be stable, for the objects at its perimeter swarm and live, never spiralling forever, or in, so must spiral out. Everything must eventually spiral out, reducing the mass that formed the hole in space.

We drift away.

DARK INFORMATION

We awaken in an infinitely dark space, a vast and empty universe.

There is a ball here. It is a sphere, so it has a size, a perimeter where its rim touches space. It has a texture and hardness. It has a colour too, in our imagination. There is already a lot of information here. Perhaps too much. What is the minimum?

The universe is reset. There is one thing here. If it has any size, its size must be relative to what? If it is the only thing in the universe, then it must be the size of the universe, infinitely big. What information does it contain? What properties does it have? Just that it is infinitely big. It is everything in every dimension. It has no edge. It is everywhere, like an all pervading whiteness. In what ways is it different than nothing? Is it different at all?

It is different because we call it one thing, and so it exists relative to nothing, a 'nothing' that was there before we created this 'everything'. So, there are two things: an empty universe, then a full one, and using time we created a contrast. That contrast is information.

Assuming time is ticking on, then we have more information than just this, as our new universe may have lived for longer than the one with nothing in.
Time and space are dimensions, and without those things, a universe can contain no information.

Could a universe with perhaps one dimension, time, but nothing else, contain information? Time or space can only be measured by a change within that dimension. In an unchanging universe, time cannot exist. It would be identical to a universe without time. It is change that makes time possible.

If things stay the same, then time does not exist. For a unchanging object, time does not exist for it.

A lonely proton adrift.

A line drawn, a filament sculpture of motion. It contains the memory of the direction in which it was pushed.

Its line is not perfect, though. Not perfect.

TRUTH

A sufficiently great intelligence can, at most, know half of the universe, as it would itself be the other half.

Even so, two additional points make this impossible. Firstly, verification of the information would require further resources. Secondly, the philosophical problem that two identical entities are the same as each other, and thus not two entities but one.

In such circumstances, the universe would not be the contents of the two entities, but the differences between them.

Two completely different things convey nothing about each other.

Two identical things convey nothing about each other.

REPLICATION

In the beginning there was pure solidity made by replication of smaller forms, but some replications were
imperfect, due to random, infinitesimal fluctuations,
and an error appeared. At that moment, in this infinite
whiteness, a sparkle of information appeared in the
difference between the whiteness and the error.

As the pure whiteness replicated further, more errors
appeared, creating a random pattern. Among these
patterns, stable patterns emerged, by chance, and
being stable, they remained, and evolution ensured
their survival over the random unstable patterns. By
chance, more complex stable patterns appeared that
could themselves replicate, and being stable and able
to replicate, these stood out and multiplied and
evolved to stand out among the random information
which continued to appear.

Errors in replication appeared even in these stable
patterns, as that which evolves into a shape requires
some instability to evolve into that shape, which by its
inclusion means that permanency is always
impossible. And so this pattern is repeated, with
regions of pure stability replicating with a slight error,
on smaller and larger scales, errors being gained on
different levels.

Pure whiteness contains no information. Pure chaos
contains no information. Pure whiteness could never
change, and so never exist, being infinitely stable.
Pure chaos would accidentally contain stable and

interesting forms. Stable forms amidst chaos must break down over time by errors in replication, but in that same chaos, stable forms could possibly reappear.

DEATH IS SILENCE

The tree branches nod in slow, cool air.
White blossom falls.
Distant metal chimes.
Smoke, delicate blueness.
Smooth water.

Peace, silence.
Nothingness.
Only those who remain forever unknown will attain
perfect peace, a zero energy state.
Nothing can be forever unknown, no star, no atom, no
neutrino, dark matter.

Orange cloth, the colour of energy.

Ripples. The wind is detected by the cloth. The cloth is
detected by the wind.

Bashō sits here, restless.
He screams.

61

LIFE IS VIOLENCE

Life is violence.

To kill large numbers of people is violence, to kill one person, to kill one beast, one cell.
To rebel is violence, to object, to push against. To defy.
To deflect is violence, to disrupt and change.
To disagree is violence, if expressed. If not expressed, then the violence is within, but palpable, as ideologies and concepts battle each other.
To change is violence. Every alteration to the universe involves an act by the powerful over the less powerful.
Pacifism is violence. An act of rebellion by the less powerful against the powerful is disruptive.
Sacrifice is violence. By injuring ourselves we cause physical damage, and emotional damage to those who are connected to us.
To postulate is violence. New ideas, new information disrupts, it releases or transforms energy. Every distant war is fuelled by every thought about it and every action concerning it.

Objects battle each other: cup against floor, comet against sun, moon against gravity, light against eyes.

The only peace is inaction, and inaction is impossible because everything that can communicate is always affected by communication at some point.

Existence is war.

MEANING

We quest for something meaningful.
We quest to achieve something worthwhile, for
something meaningful.

A meaningful thing is that which endures.
Something that others will see, and gain from.
Life is the communication of information.
When we stop communicating with others, we are
dead.
When we communicate, we live.

It is the goal of all things to communicate; to gain and
store information, and to communicate it to others.

UNIVERSE

Let us dispose of infinity, for one infinity anywhere will inevitably lead to infinity everywhere. There is no instance in the real universe of infinity, although reality will strive to move as close to it as possible. Mathematics can model infinity, but its models of infinity work to describe an ideal rather than exactly reflect reality; we could never count forever, for example, or measure anything that is infinite in size or accuracy.

We can say that space is infinite, in that there is no limit to the nothing that things can move into, but the size of the universe can still be finitely specified as the range between the things at its most extreme; this is finite. One may say that the expansion of the universe will continue forever, but as forever is infinite, this cannot be the case; like infinite space, time can be measured as the difference between the start and end of the universe in its dimension. If time were infinite, such a measurement would be impossible. Would time exist in those circumstances? No. Time is relative, as is existence.

Each of us has a unique viewpoint of the universe; you have a different view than I. This also applies to every particle and atom. Because of this, we each build up a unique picture of what the universe looks like. Our views may overlap; we might agree that the moon is over there, that the sky is blue etc., but our views can never be identical, there will always be an instance of knowledge that one of us knows that another doesn't.

This means that the knowledge about the universe that we each have is unique to us.

This might sound obvious and lacking in serious implications, but its implications are extraordinary. I might not know anything about the dark side of Jupiter; does this affect whether it exists or not? Yes. The existence of the dark side of Jupiter, or of anything, depends on our observation and knowledge of it. Our knowledge of the universe defines reality. Only what we know exists for us. Essentially, existence is relative to us, not absolute.

Of course, we can learn by communication and thus gain knowledge. Light particles communicate the existence of distant stars to our eyes, but at the same time, it is our unique knowledge that defines the reality of our universe.

What we call the objective universe is an overlap of a vast number of others communicated between all of us; a common, but not definitive or perfect, reality.

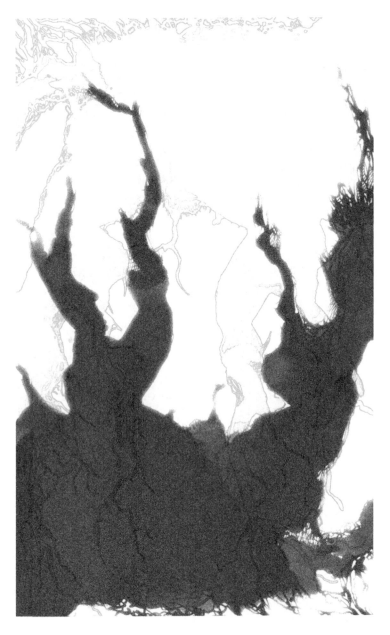

BEING

We each have a unique perspective, built from the knowledge which we acquire, and thus we exist in a unique universe of our own. Perhaps, as a result of this perspective, there is an aspect of experience to it which cannot be shared, and perhaps this is what we feel as consciousness, self-awareness, being.

If the feeling of being is the result of our unique perspective in our universe, then all things, even atoms and moons, experience this.

When we are asleep, but not dreaming, is this identical to death?

George was hard at work on the shore, assembling his sculpture, a palace of some sort, a construction of some sort.

He needed to make it, it gave him comfort. Every piece was an expression of his feelings, his needs. There was no question of why, it was simply necessary for him to make it, for his own well-being and happiness.

He assembled it in order of beauty. Things were placed in the most balanced way, a structured, symmetrical way. This felt right.

'It's beautiful,' said Lucine.

Beauty is near symmetry. Pure symmetry is limited in the information it contains, the differences between its parts. The differences need to be infinite, yet somehow, minute, like a fractal reflecting a twin soul, male and female.

The sun shone though and inside the crystals in George's palace, its rays bouncing and reflecting, running along the helical molecules, up and down with joy, dying ever so slowly, warming the transparent, polished parts. Making them sing.

Pi was there, and another...

...a feeling of deja-vu.

George stood up and looked at the sky. There were long trails, curving lines of light and shape. Concrete and crystal, rippled like snakes and dancing cubes. Reality was a sculptural form, some vast snowflake of history. All past. All future.

He looked towards the object he was building, his palace. As he moved an arm it drew a trail in space, a solid slab of arm.

The small bird, like a tiny flake in the distant sky, was forgotten, unseen. Was it there? It might be, it might not.

George looked towards Lucine: 'If time is a dimension then the future must exist, just as objects in distant space exist, yet... the existence of distant objects is dependent on the information they send, and our reception of it, and both of these factors are malleable. Reality is defined by agreement. More than that, information that is not communicated can be anything, it can extend to infinity. A sea of infinite possibility! Here, in all of us, even atoms.'

He closed his eyes.

'I will take fate by the throat;
it will never bend me completely to its will.'

- Ludwig van Beethoven (1770–1827)

DARKNESS

Ripples of sun, pulled thin into threads
through this saline sky of turquoise choke,
roads of fire thought, dragged over beds
of liquid calcium sand smoke.

Night eternal; liquorice ache
that colours each exhale rasping red,
where are your stars among these flakes
of lonely dread?

Far down, in pressure's warm lake.
Far down, in loving oil.
Far down, in golden spark's eye
and ocean's organic soil.

Here, our armies rest; weep and love,
in our nest woven from sun-wire above.

WINTER

Winter's spiny ice fingers gripped the belly of the Earth, crackling crystal fur in furrowed zigs and zags, seeking warmth to suck upon. George stood under a darkening iron-pink sky before the great bronze door, vast and smooth.

His eyes were closed, feeling the ache, like hot threads of fuse wire pulled from his frozen core, his ice heart. Oh, the iron-crusted ache. Like the grating bite of nests of teeth, grinding their flaking calcium to dust flour. The ache. Where is she?!

She is lost. She is here only as a faint red glow, a tiny warmness that caresses each atom of skin. She is lost. Somewhere distant, somewhere at the end of these steely filaments that stab into his body, pulling towards a kite, a balloon, a distant thing in a warm sky, a warm sky that is not here. The sky here was grey, flat metal, sinking to a sad, salmon hue. It was a choir singing one note, one A, that curled like Kelvin-Helm-holtz air. The ache throbbed. George opened his eyes and it subsided a little.

The heavy door before him was textured with sea creatures that seemed to writhe and curl within its liquid solid surface; knobbly shells, hideous eels, and fists of tentacles wrapped in knots and sinuous, sensual curls. George could almost taste the copper in the air that flowed over its ancient skin. His eyes could feel its chemical salt. It felt like the ache, like the zinc sting of infinite longing.

A distant church bell sang a solitary tone. He turned his head to the iron horizon and the black spire against the bleak red sky. A flight of tiny birds exploded in silent scream from behind the church like dots of scattered pepper. They whirled like ink snow around the Gothic shadow of the steeple.

Dusk. A fuzzy copper blob of sun was melting into the oil spill horizon. Oh, how that church felt spiny, with its certain graveyard and bent graves at every angle, like unshaven hairs on a dying homeless man, like George's face. Oh, how his black wire hair felt Gothic, tangled and loose, like a Romantic hero. How it ached for her thin piano fingers to run through it like a comb; to stroke his scalp in pulses, heaving.

He closed his eyes to enjoy the chemicals of ache once more. His peripheral senses were fizzing with tired-ness and uncertainty. The atoms of his skin were grey and anxious; dry, thirsty for sleep, that light liquid. Sleep. The air wine of peace. He opened his eyes, intoxicated by the sunset, by his setting sun. Night was pulling him, its ethanol coldness pulling his body towards it on strings, drawing out his ache. The harp of night. The sad harp.

Something moved in his field of vision and he looked down. On the floor, to the left of the door, there was a small, bald imp-like man. He was hunched and naked, and had dark grey skin that collected in fatty ripples at his knees and elbows. His eyes were wide and yellow, ever open. Little shivering feather wings sprouted from his silvery back. The imp looked friendly, warm even, and felt somehow familiar, like an invisible friend from childhood made real. He spoke in a squeaky voice like waxed mahogany: 'My name is Neiro, come. Come!'

The smiling imp gestured like an eager servant, and hopped forwards to the door. He placed a tiny furry hand onto the smooth metal surface and pushed. George watched the door slide silently open on its heavy hinges, sweeping its bronze hulk into shadows like silk over graphite.

The fizz of the ache was being pushed away by something warm, like chemical sandpaper, filing away the sharp metal points of the steel spider inside him. The prongs of his emotions felt rounded at the ends, somehow more attractive.

He closed his eyes to enjoy the moment, like warm water slowly, slowly caressing naked skin, creeping up from the feet, an ooze of loveliness. From the doorway, a pulse of air, soft like warm roses and clover, coughed outwards and embraced his body, like a million tiny giggling fairies, massaging every blurry sense, enticing him, pulling him forwards. He slowly opened his eyes. Neiro was crouching at the black rectangular hole with a pleasing grin, looking towards George in wait. 'Come,' he repeated happily, waving his stick arm towards the doorway.

George moved forwards, sliding and floating in liquid movements towards the warm, welcoming space beyond. The air smelled of rosewood winter fires. Forwards. Neiro bounded in, using his hands and feet in a happy gait. George followed in delicious spiral steps.

It was cloak dark inside, the comfort of nothingness. George found himself in a tunnel with smooth walls that echoed with a strange music, blurred echoes of an old song about a sandman. The sound pulsed and bounced around the hard tunnel in liquid gulps, warm toroids. He felt pulled forwards in a flow, invisibly propelled like a man in a large crowd. Ahead he could see glimpses of Neiro, the small bounding little man. The imp paused and turned to wave at George, giving an encouraging smile. His little face was lit by the square of red sunlight behind them. George stepped on, tip tap, and the light from the entrance receded into darkness, his surroundings lit only by a speckle of tiny glittering lights embedded in the upper arc of an unseen ceiling. These jewel eyes cast a mysterious and ever-pervasive light that spawned few shadows.

The air felt viscous, smooth and restful, and his cycling legs propelled him forwards as though swimming. He felt more alert now, noticing the dome and walls of this new and fascinating cavern. In the air ahead, George glimpsed a single moth-like creature fluttering in a yellow shaft of light from some distant skyward source. It danced away into the distant darkness. There was life here.

Neiro stopped up ahead and crouched patiently on the smooth floor, waiting for George to catch up.

The tunnel was wider now, perhaps two rooms wide, and the side walls were divided into evenly spaced alcoves of polished stone. In the middle of each alcove was a door; wood, metal, plastic, something frame-like, with a large rectangular window inside. Beyond the glass of these spaces, a faint green light shone out.

George stepped towards the first alcove on the left and peered in curiously. There was a room beyond with people inside, but the perspective was strangely from above, as though the window was in their ceiling. The room was dark, like evening, lamp lit. There was a family here sitting around a rectangular table; a man, a woman, and three young children. They were playing some sort of game, something like ludo, moving small pieces on a maze-like board. The youngest child, a girl, made a wrong move and everyone laughed. Her father put the piece back. George thought about his father, the games that they didn't play. Perhaps one day he would play, like this. Perhaps at one distant, forgotten time, he did.

He turned around. Each window in this cavern glowed and pulsed with life from afar, each a life, a possibility. George moved to the window opposite and peered in. A very different scene presented itself; sky, pure azure sky, with a distant valley of trees, misted blue. A silver snake of river shone in a shock of forest far below, behind wisps of white clouds, pulled thin like a mermaid's hair. Suddenly, a man appeared, flying, his arms wide in a full suit of clothes. The feeling was exhilarating. George could feel the cold mountain glacier air on his face, the warm yellow sun kissing the back of his neck. The flying man swooped and curled out of view.

George eagerly moved to the next window, and saw a party, a throng of people in nineteen-forties clothes talking and drinking fizzy wine in champagne flutes, balancing elaborate food on china plates. Somebody said something and a ripple of laughter flowed through the crowd. It parted to reveal a special guest, a happy man in a black suit and tie. It was a birthday party or something like it.

George darted across the corridor to the opposite room, curious and excited at the array of worlds on display; but here the atmosphere was more sinister. From afar, the window was dark, dusty, uncleaned for countless years. The world beyond the glass appeared black and lightless at first, but as George put his face to the pane he could perceive a dim red light, a blood glow that touched everything to form a skin. The room beyond looked like a prison cell of sorts, a bare, soiled cube. Then, movement. There was something, someone, inside; a man like a hulk of rags, a shifting mound of a man of hunched bones and dirt. George shuddered and pulled away.

He looked towards Neiro, who was sitting, utterly unconcerned, in the middle of the corridor. He seemed impatient to move on, ignorant of these fant-astic windows. George looked up at the many alcoves that lined this wide space, each window showing a different scene of possibility, all spidering towards distant future realms in ever narrowing cracks.

'Come on,' said Neiro, 'we're nearly there!'

The little imp bounced forwards on all fours, then paused, peering back for George to follow.

George noticed a tiny soap bubble, rotating in rainbow colours, then another, larger bubble pulsated into view. More bubbles appeared, and soon George was in a forest of floating orbs that formed, swarmed and waltzed around him, throbbing in the soothing air, all gently pulled forwards and away. One bubble burst, singing a single sine tone. It sounded like the church bell, and sent a shock of dread through him like an alarm. Time was short.

A pulse of ache gulped through him, from the base of his throat and flowing down through his soft being. Oh, the ache. If only its flailing wave would whip into a tear. Perhaps to cry would solve everything. But no, the sound, its metal roundness, the ache. The ache was pure beauty. Lucine was here somewhere, he could sense her optimism. She was in this space, like a shade, an electrical memory. The stars above glittered like a crystal array and sent a shock wave of blue light forwards. George walked quickly on, following Neiro.

The cavern narrowed to similar dimensions to the tunnel they began in, and the couple arrived at a closed door of smooth white metal. There was no handle, but the door was bordered with a narrow bevelled edge that could be grasped with adept fingers. Neiro reached up with his left paw, and grasped the inner bevel of the door, pulling gently to heave the door inwards. A crackle of daylight exploded around its rectangular rim making George blink and recoil. The air beyond was fresh, and a delightful pink sky welcomed George and Neiro as they stepped though.

SUMMER

The frosty grip of winter's cruel hands had gone from the mosses at George's feet, yet this place seemed strangely familiar.

Opposite the doorway, on a distant shadowed hill of salmon-grey, was a bent tree where once there was a church. The tree was burning silently, like a steady torch. The floor was verdant and rich with flowers and grasses, and the fluid air, heavy with the smell of salt-broth, was filled with flying things that skipped and darted at every micro-movement and twitch made by George. At first he thought these creatures were birds, but they twisted and undulated in such a strange way, more like fish, and as he looked, George could see that they were indeed sea creatures. The luminous air, the dappled floor, and high sky above was filled with aquatic creatures of all sorts, swimming in a warm, living metropolis.

A shell-pink light pervaded the world from all around, there was no sun, no moon. The carapace of sky appeared to be a solid glittery mass, like the inside of some vast cave.

In the upper regions of this subterranean ocean-sky, massive sharks patrolled in groups. A distant whale, vast in size, floated high like a balloon emperor, courted by young dolphin friends. A school of tiny silver fish hissed in a distant murmuration, whirling in their cyclic dance of pleasure and beauty.

In the distance was a boiling cloud, a funnel of swirling white foam, pulling down from the sky like a tornado vortex. It frothed and twisted in silence. There were things moving around it, gently floating downwards, tiny things; fish, debris, something. Tiny things being escorted from the upper sky towards the ground.

Among the grasses on the patchwork floor, George could pick out anemones and coral creatures, curious snake-like tubules of bright red, cyan, yellow hues, that snapped hand-like appendages at the air, grasping for tiny specks of nutrition. Their landscape was divided into odd regions the size of small rooms, an infinity of lozenge shaped pools or lawns, each bordered with grasses and pathways. George stepped into the cave, and onto one of these paths which snaked endlessly on, splitting into an eternal web of choices. Neiro hopped along beside him, now behaving more like some curious pet than a guide.

It seemed that most of these pools contained water, and were thick with the fine strands of an emerald green, hair-like weed. George bent down and touched the slimy surface of one pool. He recoiled in horror as he saw something below the surface, something pink and alive. It was a baby, its eyes closed and apparently asleep. The baby moved, making a gurgling noise and causing a slow ripple to flow through the thick jelly soup. George peered at the baby. It seemed so peaceful, in perfect rest. He noticed that it had frilly gill-like structures behind its ears, gills that pulsated in and out, in and out, with each liquid breath.

George stood up, and observing with newly informed eyes could discern that every pool seemed to contain babies, or at least pink masses in their liquid depths.

The patchwork of pools was broken up with hills, and occasionally, trees or tree-like structures made from calcium or stone. To the right, not far away, a clump of these trees seemed to mark a change in the environment, from its criss-cross of pools to something more like plains or broken rocks of dark brown.

George moved in that direction, picking a pathway between the pools; paths lined with the local flora of drifting sea-plants and alluring jelly tentacles. The soft floor felt like the finest sand under his feet, and his walking felt like floating, the most gentle swim. The warmth here was perfect, clothes almost unwanted in this viscous liquid bliss. The infinitely peaceful face of the baby repeatedly imposed itself on his mind. It had looked so contented in its warm pool, so restful. He froze. The baby, it was him. It was George. He knew it to be true. Perhaps other people he knew were here too, his friends Crevel, Vogh. Perhaps Lucine was here...

George darted to the nearest pool on his left, bending down and digging his knees into the delicious white sand, soft as cream. He looked into the pool and gently stroked aside the long filaments of fine green weed. Yes, there was a baby here, two in fact; yes, girls. He looked carefully at the face of one of the babies, her pulsating gills. Yes, he was sure, more sure with each passing second. Yes, this was Lucine. He drifted in thought and formed a picture of her in his mind, in their summer bed, on that final evening. She lay asleep and turned in the duvet, lemon yellow, sweet smelling, fresh.

He looked down again, and a vision formed just below the silver surface of the water. It was Lucine as she is now, dancing with a man dressed in a smart black suit. She looked sad, locked away behind a cold and silent face. The couple turned to their unheard waltz and George saw the face of the man; thin, handsome, with angular features and eyes of obsidian like dark pools. His ears were pointed. The man flicked a lightning glance of a hidden smile directly at George. George pulled away in shock and looked up to see Neiro on the opposite edge of the pool. His tiny eyes were dark. His tiny ears were pointed too.

'The man is Nyck,' squeaked Neiro, 'the king of my kind.' He smiled. 'She will be quite safe. For now. Perhaps forever.'

'Forever?' replied a startled George. 'Who is he? Where is she? How can I..?'

Neiro looked down into the pool again, the water was swirling, whirling. The scene faded.

'You will see her. You will see her, dear George. You know that, don't you?' said Neiro. 'Can't you feel her memory inside you?'

Of course, yes; thought George. He did know that he

would see her, it was a strange feeling, as though this place was somehow created by him by some sort of magic, as though the flow of his arms through this warm air had somehow brushed it into existence.

His dreaming was interrupted by a movement in the more distant pool to his right. Something was emerging from the water there, a smooth, shiny dome of pink and blue. It moved upwards, and threw back its head to show its face, blinking wide eyes at the side of its head. It was a fish, or part fish, part baby. It gulped at the air with fat lips of coral pink. Some frilly gills at the sides of its head pulsed in and out, rippling with life, breath, energy, as upwards it swam, and pushed towards the pink sky. Two tiny baby legs pushed out from the water, each ending in a rubbery fin of translucent skin.

George stood up.

The fish, as large as George, propelled itself into the air. It slowly turned in an ungainly fashion, rolling, gobbling great mouthfuls of the thick summer atmosphere. It rolled its bulbous eyes, and gently moved towards the clump of trees in the distance. A bubble floated up from the pool beneath and popped, making a sound like a little bell. Time was short.

George followed the path of the fish, marching towards the distant clump of trees, picking his way between the wet pools. Around him he noticed other fish, darting happily like pretty birds between clumps of pulsating bushes, moving in families towards the castle of trees, chattering excitedly with strange calls. As George approached the tall trunks, the path splintered into many forks, and the pools became smaller puddles, then merely damp patches of soft green-brown bog, in organic kite shapes, that emanated from the wooded area. Small twisted twigs emerged from the peaty floor like bent skeletal hands. These grew in size, pulling themselves up to become a vast cylinder of living trees, or tree-like plants. Their trunks were light brown, shiny and hard like stalactites, and they climbed to an immense height. Their sharp angular branches were tipped with clusters of dark green leaves, spade shaped and dense. They were tightly packed together, making the interior space dark and mysterious, but alluring. Life, in the form of myriad tiny fish swirled and hummed within the greenery, bouncing forwards, happily dancing around the forest like September squirrels.

George stepped into the delightful coolness of this curious wood, moving along sinuous paths of red-brown, a soft matted floor, built from the deadfall of countless branches over countless centuries. The sky above changed into a deep blanket of rich dark blue, warm like a summer evening.

The paths seemed to point and narrow in the same general direction, and the fleeting bird-fish were hopping forwards too in the same direction, bouncing towards the heart of this ancient fortress. The trees became less dense as George moved on, and a warm, white light from a moon-sun grew brighter and brighter with each step, until, stepping around a vast dark tree, its trunk perhaps two metres wide, George emerged into a field.

HONEY

The clearing was carpeted with the most beautiful soft moss of a light, spring green. The vast tree that George had just bypassed was one of several gigantic towers, evenly spaced to form a circle and mark the perimeter of this delightful place. There were twelve of them, no, eleven, for one tree was a broken stump.

A small bird, about the size of a starling, with dark feathers shocked with iridescent blue and red, flicked down at George's feet. It curiously eyed the new visitor with jerky head movements, then jumped up, and darted away with a happy chatter towards a cluster of similar birds, who were all swimming and dancing around each other like excited bees. There were people among them, wearing suits and long dresses and holding sparkling drinks in fluted glasses. Some white circular tables were scattered around the area, Victorian tables of painted iron that were stocked with white china and tea cups, tiered cake stands full of pretty little cakes, cute sandwiches of thin white bread cut into triangles, bottles of wine and more crystal glasses. Ground birds, peacocks and hens, strode among the party, pecking at crumbs, and courting.

In the middle of the group was a balding middle-aged man in a silver-grey suit. He had a thin face with angular features; his thin, fluttery eyes were etched with the creases of a lifetime of worry, yet here, he was smiling and relaxed. It was George's old university friend, Crevel. George was surprised, yet delighted, to see him, perhaps all the more surprised to see Crevel appearing so unusually happy. Contented was one thing Crevel never was. He was always worrying about the future, the world and the political situation, his health, and just about everything. George stepped quickly towards the group. Crevel saw him and welcomed him warmly.

'George! What a surprise to see you here. I'm so pleased you could come! Here, let me get you a drink.' Crevel reached for a glass filled with a fizzy yellow liquid and thrust it into George's hand. George smiled.

'Well... wow. It's really nice to see you. You know, I was just thinking about you. How are things? You look happy.'

'Ah, well, you know, I've had a bit of good luck. Can you believe it? I've just won the jackpot on the lottery. It's incredible. All of these years I've wasted worrying, and working away, and yet I could have done nothing, or could have done anything I wanted, and now - pow! I can relax, rest at last. It's like thirty years of worry are gone.'

'Huh! Well done,' said a surprised George, trying to appear as pleased for Crevel as possible at his chance windfall, trying not to think or feel anything too much, in case such thoughts might lead to envy or something harmful. He looked around at some of the other people here, all well dressed men and women, talking away politely, sipping sips, nibbling nibbles. Were these Crevel's new friends? People he had known for a long time? George didn't recognise any of them.

'Thank you,' beamed Crevel. 'Of course, it was all chance.' There was a flash of remembrance in Crevel, a memory of their friendship, a memory that perhaps he should give George some money now; but no, he could think about all of this sort of thing later, yes, later. Oh, how difficult it all is, having this money, and now having to think about friends, and how he feels about them, and how he could make them happy, or perhaps he couldn't, or perhaps he could just cause them problems. Oh. Yes. No. He could think of all of this later, carefully.

George spoke: 'I'm looking for Lucine.' Oh how he suddenly missed her! A party like this felt so dreadfully empty without her. How awful it was to be single at a party like this, like a lone cloud, like the last peacock in a deserted winter zoo, with a concrete floor cage, with only rusted leaf crumbs for company.

'Ah, Lucine, yes...' said Crevel dreamily. Oh how once he had dreamed of her too. 'You know; look!'

Crevel reached into the inside pocket of his suit and took out a photograph; old, brown and dark. He showed it to George. It looked something like a wedding photograph, but somehow uncanny and flat. Crevel was standing on the left, wearing a dark tailsuit and top hat, and smiling gently at the camera. On the right, separated by a column of air, stood Lucine. She was wearing a black ball-gown that flowed over her and onto the floor like a cascade of ink. She looked so young and happy, smiling warmly at the camera, her long blonde hair trailing loose behind her like rays of falling light. Crevel continued: 'I haven't seen her in a long time. I half expected, hoped, that she would be here.'

It was true that everyone liked her, everyone loved her. Perhaps now Crevel, with his new found wealth, felt that he could have her. The thought disturbed George.

Crevel continued dreamily: 'When was the last time you saw her?'

'Hmm...' George paused, and sank into his memory, the memory of that last evening with her. She was lying asleep in their warm, summer scented bed; the bed that was now a cold, grey November sea. Outside, an orange sky was raked with blue mackerel clouds, and there was a balloon floating there, a hot air balloon. He had gone downstairs and outside to look at it.

'I can't remember,' he said, 'but I'm sure I'll find her soon.'

He said the words, but he wasn't really sure. He wasn't sure at all. Perhaps every day would be grey from now on, but perhaps every grey has myriad colours inside. Perhaps our lives are bracketed by the extremes that we experience ourselves, and perhaps a life alone is no worse than a life with love. Perhaps the power of long-ing is as passionate as love, perhaps even more so. Life flows, up and down, and around bends. To be alone is to have the time and ability to gaze through the transparent air at everything truthfully; at what is, at what is to come, as what has been. Love is a blindfold chosen deliberately. Is that a good thing?

Crevel sighed. 'I never did find someone myself. It's just me and Orien, look.'

Crevel nodded towards his left. There was a small creature there, a little naked imp that looked exactly like Neiro. He was helping to serve at the party, taking away the empty glasses with his thin stick arms and tiny hands, replenishing the cake stands with delicious little confections, bright white cubes that looked like glowing marshmallows.

Beyond the tiny servant was a pretty house, a white walled cottage veined with ivy and with a thatched roof. The little birds were spiralling around its chimney in a gleeful dance. George became aware of some music, a lovely flowing waltz with a light curling melody that swept around the party and the guests. George noticed that his drinking glass was empty. He couldn't remember drinking it, but he had a perfect memory of the taste of the delicious liquid, delightfully sweet and sharp, yet light and refreshing on this warm day.

'Would you like another drink?' Crevel enquired, 'I have an unlimited supply.'

George watched the birds play around the eaves of the house. One bird fluttered and landed in a tiny nest made from jagged branches. Inside it was a clutch of white eggs; three small orbs, glowing white blue with an ethereal zinc-light. The eggs hatched and tiny eager mouths appeared, gaping for food from their anxious flapping parents.

The peacocks pecked and bowed. The other people at the party, these mysterious strangers, continued to talk to each other like actors. He was sure that they hadn't moved. He noticed the imp servant, Orien, take away the empty glasses with his thin stick arms and tiny hands, and replenish the cake stands with delicious little confections, bright white cubes that looked like glowing marshmallows.

'Would you like another drink?'
'Drink...' repeated George inattentively.
'I have an unlimited supply.' Crevel held up his glass, wobbling it and raising his eyebrows to ask George symbolically.
'I... yes,' said George, still enthralled by the white cottage and its little country garden.

The sky above it was streaked with an amazing rake of red clouds that arced over the cute house like malevolent fingers. The birds in the nest had grown into fledglings. One shook off a thin coat of downy feathers, causing a tiny cascade of grey particles to fall and swim away into infinity. The bird leapt, flapping off its dust crudely, then it swooped down in a wide curve below the white walls of the building, approaching the party to scavenge some crumbs from the lime green lawn. Another bird was in the nest, laying new eggs; three small orbs, glowing white blue with an ethereal zinc-light.

'There's no need to rush,' said Crevel, 'it's always eleven o'clock here.'

Oh how that feeling had pleased Crevel when he had first got here, the peace of it, now that he could rest, now that he didn't have to worry. No more worries. But oh, it was only him that didn't have to worry now. George still had worries, and Juliet, and Michael, and poor, poor Vogh. Only he could relax. Maybe he could give them some money, to help them, but who knows what the future holds? Maybe he would make them more unhappy by giving them money, and make his life more insecure at the same time? Anyway, he could think about all of this sort of thing later, yes, later. Oh, how difficult it all is, having this money.

He looked at George. He seemed distant, his eyes far away, looking at some tiny aspect of his cottage. He had seemed so happy with Lucine. How sad it was that he had lost her. Of course, he must be lonely. How sad that such things could exist in this perfect world on this perfect day.

Crevel sipped some of the delicious nectar. A glow of pleasure swelled in his head, a warm explosion like a golden orb of expanding honey-joy.

George felt lonely here. The place and the people seemed to be made from thin plastic, or glass; some-how fake. The happy little birds seemed to be the most alive things in the garden. A pang of longing pulsed through his chest. He felt like a cave, a wet cave in the middle of Wales, or an empty Russian church. Crevel's words echoed inside him, bouncing off the stony walls and around the smoking candles; yet, there was some warmth, a tiny spark of warmth, in the darkness.

The back of the house had a somewhat decrepit garden, and clusters of rough weeds, and the same broken-bone trees bled from there towards the dark rim of this circular field. The distant woods beyond looked spiky and oppressive, black; yet in that black, somewhere in its centre was a particle of whiteness too, a tiny lovely light, like the spark.

The little birds had become distressed by something. George looked closely and saw that there was a man on the wall, climbing the ivy like some hideous spider, no not a man, an ape-like creature, with short legs and long arms and covered in black hair. The ape was creeping towards the bird's nest and reaching inside to harvest the eggs. The birds were screeching and swooping at him like biplanes. The ape waved at them while grabbing the glowing eggs and placing them with great care into a pendulous satchel that was slung around his neck. The last egg was deposited, and the ape leapt free of the ivy, jumping to the ground and landing on all fours with a deft thump. He cast a few furtive eyes at the ignorant party guests, not noticing George, and then scurried to the back of the house, its spiny garden, and into the dark woods beyond.

The birds were gone, lost, away. Gone like dreams upon waking, now invisible shades. George felt uncommonly sad. He could feel those eggs, their lightness and beauty, kidnapped away by the brutish creature; those tiny balls, like little children, in the bag, siblings of hope being pulled sideways to drown in the inky coldness of the black woods. Away they flowed. Away like candle smoke. He had to follow them.

'I must go,' he said hurriedly. He handed his empty glass to a confused Crevel and immediately jogged off in pursuit of the ape.

'Well, I...' said a startled Crevel as George left.

Crevel let out a little sigh, sad to see George leave. There were so few people here that he saw regularly, well, there were none really; he didn't even see much of George. He supposed that now, now that he had enough money to relax and not worry about working, he could spend as much time as he wanted with any-one; but then, would they want that? And would they have the time? So much of his life was spent working; in pursuit of money, of peace, of hope. Now he had it. Now he had everything, infinity. He was on a separate golden plateau now, unreachable. He looked towards the other guests, the holographic automatons sipping their pretty drinks and chatting away in an eternally pleasant babble. What was there to do now? He wondered what it would feel like to be a holographic automaton guest at an ever-lasting party held for a stranger.

The garden at the back of the house was coarse and made of long matted grasses like tufts of unkempt hair. Up ahead, the forest sank into darkness. In it, George could see a tiny flicker bob up and down. The glowing eggs, magically visible through the bag of the thief, were singing out their happy light.

BLOOD

Boom. Like a gulp. Like a thunderous elephant's fall, a deep resonating pulse radiated from some distant dark heart, from some place over there, flowing across the woods in blood-soaked waves towards George. A deep and primitive sound. To be feared.

The woods were darker than before, draped in shadows of liquid midnight under a flat sky that offered little illumination. The paths were shaped like lightning rays, as if carved by an explosion of energy that originated in the sun-moon grove of Crevel's eternal party. The air had cooled and was scented like blood, a scent which flowed from the beating heart of the forest up ahead.

The ape-man in front remained barely visible, like a darting shadow that crisped and cracked along pathways of dry bracken and filaments of spiny vegetation. He could be seen primarily by the eerie glow that emitted from his bag of eggs. The curious light acted as a beacon, guiding George's way into the woods.

The air grew thicker, rustier, as did the light, like a winter sunset, painting everything orange red. A sound could be heard, a regular throbbing, like blood soaked ears, thumping like a heartbeat, making every leaf shudder. Thump. Throb. Heaving in deep drones. There was a light ahead, a fire flickering among the cold, black trees. The ape had reached a clearing, and George, creeping behind as quietly as the crisp vegetation would allow, followed. He stopped behind an

107

ancient twisted tree, gripping its rough wrinkled skin to peer with trepidation at the scene before him.

In the middle of the clearing was an organic throne, hewn crudely from a tree stump and flanked by two flaming torches of dancing yellow. On the throne sat a huge, black-haired ape wearing a crown of bent metal. Around the edge of this court were many apes, seemingly a few, at first, but it became apparent that a large crowd was present, their red-dot eyes blinking like fireflies in a hulking sea of black shapes, humanoid outlines that swayed, groaned, hummed, with a primitive, animalistic, babble.

The ape that George had been following stopped in front of the throne and bowed his head, then his body, to the ground, spreading his arms wide before his king. The crowd of apes began to chatter and whoop loudly. Some began to jump and scream with a frightening barbarism, baring hideous yellow teeth that shone in the flickering firelight.

The king raised his left wrist and the noise abated. He seemed tired, slow, compared to the young apes of his court, but not old. George saw that many of the creatures here were thin and unhealthy, even emaciated. They gazed at the new arrival and his glowing bag of plunder with lustful eyes; staring, salivating, greedy, envious. The chatter of the court abated, and the air became deathly quiet, its sound populated by the breaths of a thousand violent beasts, two thousand staring eyes. George breathed extra quietly; tiny-mouse breaths to emit the bare minimum of sound.

To the right of the king stood a young ape, a prince or rival perhaps. His right claw was flexing, his eyes pulsating, wide and narrow as he stared at the bowing ape.

Boom. A deep drum sounded from some unseen source, sending a gulping throb through everyone's chest. With each of its warm liquid waves a notch of intellect clicked down, an angle of reason became sanded smooth; sanded down towards the jagged granite of base emotions.

The lustful eyes of the prince flicked towards the bag of eggs, then back to the gaze of the new arrival. The two apes locked eyes in a stare of power. The crowd began to chatter, quietly at first like the tick tick of a thousand distant trains running on metal tracks, then louder like the click click of a million black beetles flapping upturned on a hard kitchen top. In slow waves everyone began to chant, then faster and faster, rasping and rattling, rattling and rasping.

The ape prince began to creep forwards, slowly like a stalking cat, arm before arm, eyes locked upon the ape before the king. His quarry took off his satchel and let it fall.

The ape prince raised his right claw, showing its hideous jagged fingernails. The drum boomed; and he leapt at his target.

The crowd began to scream in a frenzy as the two fought, spectators taking sides and leaping with wild energy. The two apes bit each other, each sinking knife teeth into the other, letting black blood drip like treacle, spraying the arena with its iron stink. Claw ripped flesh, eyes wide with savagery. Both apes paused, panting, bleeding, then leapt at each other once more. The prince ape sunk his teeth into the thigh of the other. His victim twisted and rolled onto his back, pulled free, and grasped at an ear, tearing it off. The prince then grabbed the thin arm of the other ape, gripped it with both hands, then snapped it in two with a hideous bloody crack. The victim yelped as the prince raised his left paw to the high sky, above the head of the injured ape. Time slowed.

A new pulse of sound flowed from the deep drum, gliding like a dark, warm breeze over the crowd. The eyes of the apes gaped wide, all control was gone, all reason, all rational thought, all consciousness. Only bestiality remained, raw and senseless. The hand came down onto the face of the injured ape; he fell. Then a foot crunched onto his neck, and it twisted to tear the thin flesh. Blood, this time white blue, glowing like the eggs, warm and thin, spurted up and over the killer, spraying him with its glittering sparkle of stars. The glowing liquid poured over the floor from the gaping wound. The injured ape gargled and uttered a shriek from his moribund body, vomiting up a bucketful of his life energy, then lay down, trembling with ever decaying ticks, like a watch spring winding down to a cold stop.

There was utter silence. George froze, shaking in cold shock at the horrific sight. The crowd, too, were still.

The only movement came from the victor, scarred and bloody with black blood, with white blood. He was panting in and out. He flicked out a tongue to lick his salty lips as his breathing slowed. He sniffed, then looked towards his king.

The king was watching calmly. He nodded, and slowly moved his right hand, reaching down into the ink of shadow that clothed the area around his throne. His hand emerged holding a black lump object, like a large oval rock the size of a head. He threw it forwards to the floor, a gift for the victor. The winning ape limped towards it and picked up the object, watched by all of the assembly. With both hands he cracked it apart. It was white inside, like bread, yet there was something else embedded in there, a black stick thing, cold and evil, something that radiated a force of ice around the arena that George could feel in his shoulders, in his arms, in the wet sockets of his eyes.

The ape pulled it out; it was a dagger with a blade of infinite blackness that radiated an anti-light of death. The ape pulled it out and gripped its hilt, then waved it in an elaborate curl in the air before him. The dagger pulsed with darkness, shining an all-enveloping black that sucked away every morsel of life and energy. The crowd of apes were awestruck, transfixed by the knife in a zealous ultra-silence.

George was trembling with fear. He took an instinctive step backwards, away from this terror, and 'crack!' A twig snapped with the loudness of a screaming bell. The holder of the dagger instantly turned to look dir-

ectly at George, the tiny eyes of George, the tiny terri-
fied eyes that had been spying on their savage scene.

The ape thrust the dagger skywards and hissed
through his broken, yellow knife teeth.

Boom.

George's jelly legs quivered into action and he turned
and ran. The ape screamed and bounded towards
George, dragging the crowd with him.

MIDNIGHT

In panic, George darted along black, tangled paths. Leg over leg, pushing, thrusting, swimming through forests of twisted ivy, knee-high carpets of ferns, nests of dark sticks like crisp needles that cracked and hissed like the bones of the pursuing apes; the violent apes, salivating and hissing towards his pulsing veins, hot with blood and panic.

The path was lost, abandoned; the best way to escape was to head deep into the forest. Deep. Deep into inky blood darkness, the gulf of shadow and rasping barbs. Deep into the web of vines that pulled and dragged at George's clothes like eager witch claws. In and out sagged his heavy lungs, his burning throat. Escape, he must escape.

He burst through a wall of tight hedge and suddenly found his surroundings clear, the vegetation forming something like a passage. The floor was soft and silent. He ran along it. The end of the path was a junction, he could turn left or right. A distant church bell sounded; a dull ring that pulsed in and out, like a warm saline sea current. Eleven fifty five. In the star sky, a razor blade whipped through a white cloud horizontally, slicing it in two.

He turned left, jogging, his limbs fizzing with pain, his burning muscles screaming for cool oxygen. In the distance behind him, the sonorous cackle of ape screams echoed through the wintery winds.

He reached another junction. There was an alcove cut into the hedge at the end containing a statue of white marble, a man draped in a heavy cloak, his right hand clasping a scythe. His other hand gripped a clock on a chain, black enamel hands making the hour on a background of nacre. Eleven fifty six. A burgundy velvet rose shuddered and shocked into white-grey, its ash petals falling to the ground. He turned right this time.

His pathetic legs slid across the grass, his running now a dizzy walk. An opening appeared in the left wall of the hedge, then a second gap on the right. Left felt like forwards. He went through the gap into a small circular garden, its exact design barely visible in the night light. He heard the sound of running water, and in the centre perceived a fountain shaped like a fish, like the bulbous fish he saw emerging from the pool earlier, but now cast in a gold metal. A trickle of water dripped from its mouth into a shimmering pool that reflected a white disc; a clock face. Eleven fifty seven. A thin spider web shook, then crisped into taut mica, hard spines of grey sugar-glass. It exploded into a billion dust fragments, sending a cloud of scent, of heavenly sweet confection, over the garden lawn.

Ring. Ring. Ring. There was no way out of this garden. George stepped back into the main passage and jogged along, past the gap on the right, to the end of the passage, which veered left into an zigzag arcade of bushes. Down the centre of this passage was a line of cypress trees. George moved forwards, snaking between the trees which emitted a delicious pine smell. The walls of this arcade featured regular gaps through which George could see new passageways, new directions and options. There: in the shadows, an ape? A panther? He moved on, now stronger, his lungs having drank deeply some of the air wine that his legs and arms had begged for. He swam past the branches, letting the young cypress fingers brush his face with utmost delight.

The end of this arcade was semi-circular, a concave area, perhaps ten metres in diameter with a floor of delicate lime-green grass, short and neat like a bowling lawn. In the centre of the lawn was a bent tree, dead and hunched like a hanged man, a twisted monolith. From it swung a dented clock on a rusty chain, an iron clock whose heavy hands choked and coughed at every minute they heaved through, grating their ancient gears in eternal pain. Eleven fifty eight. A moth exploded into a thousand brown crumbs, a thousand meteors thrown into the infinite black of vacuum space.

Far behind him, a boom sounded, like distant thunder, a dim light in a vast cave, a swallow of vodka on an icy morning. There was nothing here in this maze, nothing but night and coldness and beauty. Beauty, yes, organic rococo, Art Nouveau, everywhere, in loving curls, reaching out for something close, something almost within reach. There were no people, no other people or living things, just paths, pointers to something forwards, something nouveau. The bent rococo hands were pointing the way; to her perhaps, no, surely, to Lucine, yes. That must be it, the goal beyond the matted vines and hedges, through the tight webs of this viscous night, around the clumps and clusters, the rocks and pathways. She is up ahead, waiting there in her cave, her den, her palace of dreams and destinations. She is waiting just beyond, just beyond the walls. Touch your face to the wall, she is on the other side of the paper, within feeling distance, within the empathic range of water through the walls of the thinnest, most transparent glass.

The arch of hedge had four rectangular holes, four possible exits. Which, which?! George picked the one ahead and slightly to the right and walked down the pathway there, a new tube of green roof, covered with boughs of a twisted wood, hanging with dead roses. The air was rose scented too, beautiful pink, but the light remained a dark gloop, an all embracing liquid shadow. This pathway was long and waved like a snake, left and right, then, gaps appeared on each side as it came to an end, dead with a fall of rocks that looked as if a mountainside had miraculously collapsed into it. A gentle water, like tears, glistened on the rocks.

George looked left, then right, through the gaps at each side. Both paths looked similar to this one, although the path to the right had less of a roof, and there was some discernible starlight falling to the floor in his near-field of vision. The left path remained dark, but somehow warmer, more cosy. The rose scents flowed around him, entrancing, alluring. The darker path seemed to be calling to him like a siren, pulling his weak senses towards it. He looked right again to the lighter path, to its cool crispness. Right;

yes, this must be the way. He turned right, stepping through the rectangular hole cut in the hedge, moving forwards along the short tunnel, the few dark metres formed of helical rose branches. They soon gave way, in bent finger filaments, to a midnight sky of pinprick stars and ice-fresh air.

The path curled left in a wide, even arc, as though it were circular. The hedges here were less leafy, and dark and hard, and as George stepped onwards, the hedge achieved a less organic and more calcined form, becoming stony and brittle, like petrified remains. Clouds of tiny flies swam around the bushes, seeking micro-scraps of organic matter on these spiky fragments. The grass floor too, began to bald and blacken, growing longer and flatter, like charred straws. There was a flickering light up ahead, and the path turned sharply right into a small enclosure containing a bright fire.

George stood at the entrance to a square garden the size of a large room. A burning tree was slumped at its centre, its yellow fire hot on his heatless violet skin. The rough hedge fell away in height, crumbling and tumbling to knee level, giving George his first clear view of his surroundings since leaving the distant wood. He stood on top of a hill with a vast panorama. A vast swathe of cyan-blue formed a great arc in the night sky overhead, like great glowing arms, and all around he could see that he was in the midst of a vast organic maze that seemed to spread like an infinite web to the horizon in every direction. The ground rippled and rolled to his left and right, undulating like the manifolds of a great brain, cut with a million paths, choices, options, destinations. The blinding light of the fire made it impossible to see beyond it. This tree, bent and carbonised like a skeletal hand in agony. Leaves like black plates fell from it screaming, tumbling dead to the ground. The eternal clock. Perpetuum mobile. Eleven fifty nine. A baby weeps, black oil tears running from the corners of its eyes, falling into a sea of liquid fire, rippling outwards in rings of sinusoidal sound, a pure hum of gold like electron orbits at supraphotonic speed. Cracks in the plates form, rip open, tearing their porcelain with a wounded dinosaur's cry, lament. The pinprick stars rocket away at hyperspeed, slicing white laser-rays into the dome of reality.

The only way out was back; back along the mangled graphite path, back to the verdant shoots of organic reality, back crunching over the grass of the winding arc, back to the rose scents, the alluring pink scents and the fallen rocks painted with tearfall. George stepped from the right hand doorway to the dead end of fallen rocks beneath the arms of the tangled rose stems. The stones were still wet, their hard skin moist and salty. Perhaps these rocks were once a statue, a creature once admired and now decayed into fragments, remnants of something that might have been great, perhaps a great masterpiece or teacher. Now they lie majestic in their self-made bed, perhaps more beautiful than ever in this ultraromantic grotto.

Ahead of George was the dark gateway, the shadowed tunnel lined with roses, tantalising. He stepped though, moving quickly. He had to escape this labyrinth. It was dark, but the matted vines overhead had many holes, affording an attractive view of the night sky beyond, the blue-cyan arcs like vast ribbons, a moonbow. The heavy scent of roses fell away, replaced with something fresh, alcoholic, like the scent of lemon static electricity, and the hedges began to grow neater and more ordered. The tangled arms of rose vines became less and less dense, drawing electric lightning patterns as they fell away, first in roads, then paths, then veins, to fine hairs, to nothingness, revealing the infinite cavern of the night sky above.

Navigating in a reflection of the other pathway, this curving path turned sharply left into a square garden, although this one had no fire at its heart, no majestic views or sensational drama. In the middle was a large sculpture of black wood, like a fist bent over, but monkey shaped; a hulking ape. It was fragmented, constructed from bent strips, like rib bones, and more air than solid. An ape, frozen in time, in gentle starlight, casting a criss-cross of shadows over the grey green grass, the air breath floor of this quiet chamber. The right hand of the sculpture stretched out and clawed at the soil of the neat garden. Its cowering head gripped something in its teeth, something hanging like a thread. George moved into the serene scene, his mood subdued, almost peaceful. The maze now seemed deserted. He now seemed alone.

Alone. The scream of the distant apes was now silent. Crevel was a murky memory of childhood sunshine. Lucine; she was nowhere, even her memory was asleep.

The stars watched George from afar with their tiny silver eyes, watching the lost man in the maze. The distant edges of his world were now pure blackness in all directions, a furry nothing, like creeping ink bleeding towards the little man.

George stepped into the room. The ape sculpture was biting a chain which was gently swinging. The chain was made of grey stone, and made a horrific clinking clatter as it moved, like a thousand bones in a windstorm.

The poor church; the poor distant bell with its dull ring that pulsed in and out, like a warm-saline sea current. The sea flowed grey with smoke, curling coldness like a swarm of micro ice crystals, like frozen tears.

The chain ended in a clock, a cube of stone. George moved closer and gripped the chain with his left fist. He felt comfortable, shielded from the world beneath the wooden carapace of this hulking statue. The face of the ape was not savage but calm, resigned. Any savagery was locked away, turned into art, frozen into a three dimensional form of beauty. This place was beautiful, the whole place. Yet, the ink void crept on.

The poor statue of white marble; the man draped in a heavy cloak, his right hand clasping a scythe, now crackled with black lines, pulled into thick fissures, then exploded into dust and the void of nothing. Eaten by entropic forces.

There is always hope. There are always stars, casting their silver eyes through slits. The gaze of loving gods. The cube clock turned as George held the chain tightly.

The poor fountain shaped like a fish; cast in a gold metal, dripping a trickle of water from its mouth. The water was dry, a flow of running sand that coughed from the gaping metal lips. The sand made the metal sing and ring like a gong as each tiny glassy cube crashed into its bronze surface. Each collision was a cry of pain, hope, anguish.

It was a stone clock, a dead clock, its face permanently set.

The poor burning tree; bent and carbonised like a skeletal hand in agony. Its poor leaves like black plates, falling from it screaming, tumbling dead to the ground. They were cool now, shining black like oil, breathing slowly in their sick-beds, weeping at the memory of their youth on the tree, when it lived fresh and young, that light green morning of childhood.

Midnight. A gaggle of shattered umbrellas cackled like bat witches: cak cak cak cak cak. Blackness consumed everything. George found himself falling.

CHILDHOOD

George was falling down a tunnel of some sort, swallowed by the earth, as though a trapdoor had opened up beneath him. He awoke face down on a hard floor, his limbs splayed in all directions like a murder victim, the long strands of his black hair bleeding over the tiles like a leaking octopus. He cracked open his eyes and pushed down to heave his torso upright.

He was lying on a smooth tiled floor, of plastic tiles with a checker-board pattern; white and something like turquoise. The floor was not clean; each cloudy tile was edged with a dark grime. It was cold. He was in a dark room, it was night time, but he could see by the light from a window to his distant left. He stood up. He was in a farmhouse kitchen from perhaps the nineteen fifties, perhaps the nineteen thirties. A wooden-edged window looked out onto a night garden, and a certain moon, somewhere unseen beyond, was casting a bright light over the scene, illuminating a familiar worktop, a square porcelain sink, an old kitchen table with a Formica top, and two rickety wooden chairs. It was George's childhood home.

The alcove opposite contained the stove, an old wood-burning stove of iron black. It was unlit. There was no sight of the hideous tip-tapping cockroaches that used to huddle in their chattering masses beneath its glowing warmth. The sink beneath the window, eternally plugless, was empty. A cube of green household soap sat on the draining board.

He stood up in the cold night air, his shoes crisping on the hard floor. He turned gently and touched the back of one of the wooden chairs, caressing the warm past. It was soft and smooth, sanded by a million hands over countless decades. This old friend, so long forgotten. This simple chair, worn and comforting that creaked at every quiet breakfast, and waved its uncertain bones under one of the many old family guests on Christmas Eve, those busy nights of lights and laughter. Here it was, here in its perfect imperfection, dents and shades exactly as he remembered them. Here it was, waiting here, in his old kitchen, here in the moonlight. It wasn't even very dusty. The whole room, in its invisible mist, was here as though waiting; in a waiting room of the past, waiting for things to change, for the grown ups, for real life to arrive, for the dream to fall, for childhood to go, to exhale, drop, particle by tiny young particle.

But this place was always there, somewhere, somewhere inside, sealed in an egg shell in his inner core, protected like a hen's yolk in a thin glossy membrane of something lovely. Sealed in its ark, back then, and held close and forever since.

Everything was still. Calm like a grey blue photograph. The room was more like a ghostly daguerreotype than a museum exhibit, and nice. The walls, the layout of the room, buzzed his senses to say hello, welcome back old friend.

While he was thinking, something extraordinary happened. The door to the back garden was to his left, white painted wood in six panels, and bolted shut. A glowing boy suddenly appeared there, running into the room in complete silence, right through the closed door. He was made from a bright transparent light of white-blue, shadowless and beautiful, and yet moved completely naturally, running in as though he had been playing outside, without a single concern for the darkness, without seeing or acknowledging George. In a few seconds, the boy's ethereal body ran right through George and out of the room through the closed door to the hallway. After an initial flicker of shock at this wonderful sight, George smiled, sparked by happy feeling. Of course, the boy was him; the young George.

He pulled open the door into the hallway and stepped out. A scent of applewood and rose coke floated around, warm wax, the soft evocations of distant memory. The front door was opposite, at the end of the hallway, panelled with lots of little square windows of textured glass, and little locks and a brass chain that he used to hook on, unhook, hook on, unhook, to peer at the world outside. Beyond was a road that ran left and right, a carriageway for the few cars that hissed by. The railway line was just beyond, perhaps fifty metres over a stubble field of hardy grass pecked with dandelion warts. The trains weren't noisy, a gentle hum, left to right, like the flow of sea over pebbles that could wash an anxious child to sleep.

The stairs were on the left, running down towards the front door like a waterfall, and with a bannister that could be sat astride and slid down with great joy on

127

spring mornings. He never fell down the stairs in all of the years of running and jumping up and down them. The joy of stairs, the little hills in our houses. The youthful elation of darting up and down. How horrific a bungalow or flat would be, that jail of the old. The hallway was now lit gently with a distant starlight glow from the rectangles of light in the front door. Oh, to step out into his childhood street, to touch the floor and stroke it. Oh, to touch the small lawn at the front of the house, to kneel there or lie on it, front down, heartbeat touching the cold earth, arms wide over the vast soil earth, the great ball of the world. Would the people there, the houses there, be there as he remembered?

To his right was a door to the back room, the colder room where the old television sat with its chunky buttons. The furniture was all wooden looking, all dark brown and polished. A second door along led to the front room, with its deep wool carpet, golden like strands of pulled wheat, warm and rich, like a lion's fur. A flickering light shone out of that doorway, the movement of a person; the boy must be in there.

George moved forwards and stepped in. The carpet was exactly as he remembered. Opposite the door, at an angle, was a cabinet of red wood and glass, filled with wine glasses and fine cups. Those were used only at Christmas or for special family occasions. The scent was of pine needles and flowers, the delicious fine ferns, ultradelicate fronds that were kept in four or five pots on a small book cabinet to the left, just in front of the arc of the bay window at the front of the house. Yes, there it was, the book cabinet, waist high with stubby legs and glass slide doors, containing a rag-bag of books, mostly leather bound red books with yellow musty pages and tiny Times Roman letters; how to write short hand, sewing, some children's books with tattered dust jackets made from a strangely waxy paper, with oddly faded colours and black writing on a yellow background.

In the middle of the room was George as a child, kneeling down and playing with a toy car, a small glowing toy. Ah, that car. He'd forgotten all about it. All of the toys that he once had, those magical things given at every Birthday and Christmas, and so wanted, so desired and enjoyed, and yet at some point they all faded away, all gone, given, forgotten. For every lost toy there is lost a part of a child tied to it, a thin thread of light that connects us to each object like a friend, a play-mate. Tiny jigsaw pieces of our souls are linked to these things that we once loved and that were lost, forgotten among the rush of other people, books, the complicated jungles of adulthood. Those jigsaw pieces inside us shrink, yet, there is always a hole there that remembers, a hole that shines and speaks: 'Hello...? Where are you...? Do you remember me...? Can we play...?' And we have forgotten it, we have said 'no' too many times. The time for toys has gone. The toys are lost and far away, and all we have is that little jigsaw hole inside us that will never be filled, or feel warm again.

But today it does feel warm, because here is the missing piece. Here is the lost car, right in front of George.

The boy drove it along the patterns in the carpet, the roads in the pattern, like George used to do. How happy the boy looked. How happy the car looked, with its boy. That's my car, thought George. That was his happiness. That is mine... but it was only once his. It is not his toy any more. Like all of his toys, it fell to the floor and he let them fall; and he walked on to something else.

A man's voice spoke: 'Would you like a drink?'

It came from the left. George turned to see a man standing in the doorway. A pale man with short black hair, slick and pulled back, and dark eyes of hypnotic void. He was dressed in a dinner suit, with a white shirt and dark tie, and holding a conical glass in each hand containing what looked like sherry. He moved one glass towards George. George took it. He noticed that the man had pointed ears, then recognised the man as the one he had seen in the pool of water, the man who was dancing with Lucine.

'Ah, I've seen you! In a vision; you were dancing with my love, Lucine.'

The ache reappeared in a gulping wave, an explosion of liquid spaghetti filaments emanating from his core, their barbed tips tingling with electricity. Oh, how could something distant, a longing of loss be somehow so warm, somehow so pleasing yet unpleasing at once. What was it in the undersea storm of these feelings, this chemical swirl that made want so enticing as a feeling. The wanting of nothing, the romance of the emptiness. George needed a stab of pleasure, right there. He sipped the sherry. It was deliciously sweet, a heat glow of supreme pleasure. A pulsation of pure summer flowed from his stomach, up through his throat, to his head, and sat there, basking on a dreamy meadow beneath a gong-beat sun. Its joy subsided.

'Good, isn't it?' said the man. Nyck, that's what Neiro had called him. Nyck took a sip.

George looked to his right, at the playing boy. The boy was now less bright, his glow mirroring the glow of this magical fluid in George's veins. The boy pulsed in and out of brightness, playing with his toy, which was also pulsing in and out of brightness. Then, as the feelings of pleasure dissipated, so too did the sight of the boy, flickering then fading to brown, to a sad brown dust. The smell of the room changed as its delicious fresh pine scents faded into potato dust, dessicated loss. Dessicated dust.

'Don't worry,' said Nyck 'it is all part of the natural cycle. These things swell and fade, then swell again, round and round.'

Music began to play, a tinkling waltz like a music box, and George found himself dancing with Nyck, turning around clockwise, then anti-clockwise in little curls round and round.

The music sang of sand. Sand, the tears of time. The room began to look more and more brown, the walls taking on the appearance of an ancient photograph. As he turned he looked at the mantelpiece above the fire. His parent's clock was there under its lovely glass bell, a golden clock with four rotating brass balls that spun clockwise then anti-clockwise; round and back. The clock didn't look right though, it wasn't the same shape as he remembered... although he wasn't sure what shape it should be. The memory was blurred. Now it was shaped like a church, a Gothic church with a tall spire. George fixed upon the clock church, trying to look at it while Nyck pulled him round, round in whirls and whirls. Everything felt pulled into a whirl-pool, dragged like many colours of paint into streaks. He blinked and tried to fix upon the clock, the shadow statue of the church, the soot glitter of tiny birds that perpetually swarmed around its spire.

He looked up. The ceiling had become a glistening mirror, a whirl of water that curled and spiralled like the music, round and round in dizzying circles. There was something beyond it, something he could see beyond the sky. The ceiling wasn't showing a reflec-tion, but a world beyond, a new place, somewhere else. Then he saw a face, a huge face in the sky loom-ing over the scene. It was him, his face from the sal-mon-sky world, his face looking at himself waltzing round and round and round. The music kept repeat-ing, over and over, pulled thick and thin, in and out, warm and cold, round in cyclic echoes. George felt that he had to pull away. He had to escape this dance. He pushed at Nyck with weak arms, limp like bread dough. He pushed with both jelly arms and leaned back, pulling from Nyck's grip, leaning away, pulling his body back like toffee on a hook, stretching his gooey form. He felt that he was moving up, upwards and away, so slowly, but his efforts were working. Back, and up, like a drowning swimmer at the bottom of a winter pool. Back, gasping for the air beyond the sky. Up through the black air, this ice choke air, thick with salt ink. Up he pushed, pushed, swimming upwards towards something new and fresh. Up, up, his body was free, only his legs were now stuck, pulled to thin rubber ropes. Up, yes. He was nearly at the ceiling, the skin of sky. Up; and bursting through the membrane of space, the surface of the water. Through and out.

THE LAKE

Exhale. Pure relaxation bliss. Floating. Floating in a lake of smooth glass paradise. Above him, the sky had cast an arc of stars, a billion ice-diamond prickles, glittering in the vast panoply of the entire universe. The air was warm and cool, pure, and seasoned to perfection as he floated, face up, in this perfect dark water, this smooth mirror that reflected the infinite glitter of the night sky.

Pure relaxation bliss, like the creak of blood in your ears after a stretch. Exhale.

He became aware of something moving, in the air, a glow of light. To his right was a tiny flying thing, a flickering speckle. He turned his head to see a mayfly with the tiny body of woman, her entire body casting a beautiful pink glow that reflected double in the plate glass water, dark and deep and smooth. She flew towards him, and he saw that there were others, two others; one shining a beautiful powder-blue light, and the other yellow-green. The three flies flew to his floating body, smiling and playing around his face like young children.

They sang a gentle tune: 'Deee tooo. Da-deee tooo dohhhray daaa'.

Gentle clouds above, grey against the black void of starborn space, drifted in delicate breaths, pulling their wool into the thinnest vapours. There was no perceptible wind at all here, just up there, and even then the most gentle of movements.

'You're pretty little things,' George's soft voice said. The little flies giggled. The red one said: 'weee arrr-e the pixxx-els, we can creee-ate airrr-nything.'

The little pixels floated around and waved their tiny arms. A little string of bubbles appeared where the arms moved, tiny bubbles of rainbow colours that mixed and swirled. The bubbles made tiny little sounds as they popped; tiny little tinkly bell sounds.

The pixels laughed and flew up, up in a helical dance, up towards the stars like living fireworks. They blinked and flickered, creating a dazzling speck of colour, of all colours. Their three bodies looked like one thing, like a star candle, a tiny light dancing in and out and rotating a rainbow of hues. He lost them among the vast glitter background of the universe. All of the stars looked like pixels, all glittering and shivering in their ice velvet night. He noticed that the dark space between them wasn't simple blackness, not a nothing-ness, but a coat for each star, accepting every glow and shimmering too, in and out. The entire panoply of the stars appeared like a dancing screen.

What was this reality? This place. Could this world be sliced into sections, tinier and tinier, into hard balls of atom, tiny balls hugged together like refugees, not let-ting the world pull them apart, tightly hugged against the extreme winter of the universe, eyes clamped shut against the horror of black holes. This place seemed too soft for such things, soft like a world of candyfloss projections. Soft like a cloud settee made from hope.

George lifted his hand from the water and looked at it, carefully observing every detail, every fold, line, and skin road of his life. Was this any more real than those stars? Was his body any more real than the world around him? He looked around a little more. Does this lake have a shore? It did. The dark sky fell in a dome from inky blackness to a misty blue of electric air. In front of its horizon was an undulating silhouette of land. There was a light on the land up ahead, in the direction his feet were pointing; there was a building there with brightly coloured lights.

George noticed that he was moving, being pulled towards that land with an imperceptible current.

The building on the shore was a church, high up on a hill, the same church he had seen countless times. Its stained glass windows were lit up brightly against the coal darkness of the island; segments of red, green, blue. Dazzling patterns and combinations. He was sure that in the light, he could see a figure, just the vague outline of a person in front of the church, a woman calmly standing there. He was sure that it was Lucine, exactly standing as he saw her in Crevel's old photo-graph, wearing the black ball-gown; but there was so little light, so little. A warm blackness drowned everything here, and its depths were home to only the tiniest speckles of brilliant light.

George moved his arms in great wheels and pulled in his legs, tumbling to face forwards. He began to swim towards the shore.

A distant bell sounded, the echo of an echo. In the velvet darkness of the sky, where the sky touched the land, a tiny azure strand formed, a crack of white, as thin as the thinnest hair, a fibre of pearl-chain atoms, razor sliced through horizontal air.

George pushed the water glass behind him with delicious cyclic sloshes.

A second bell sounded. The sky quaked and shivered, like ducks fresh from the rain. The diamond stars blinked, in love with their arc of night, and the arc of the earth far beneath their heavenly domain.

He was coming closer to the shore. The church on the hill had sunk below the dark shadows of the land before him. The shadows formed stark angular shapes against the blue ink sky, like tree palms, huge bent hands, twisted wrestlers. He could hear a faint lap lap of the crystal water as it stroked the land.

Somewhere, a metal mallet wrapped in leather, eased into a bell once again, deforming the bronze in rippling undulations to send a radiant exhale of sound across the countryside, a flight of tiny fireflies, tumbling and shrinking in a sinusoidal swarm.

George reached the shore, a gentle slope of soft sand. He crawled onto the beach and pulled his body up, brushing off the electric dusts of water and sand to leave his clothed body dry and comfortable. A faint blue-grey starlight from behind provided illumination, and he found himself standing in a small concave inlet bordered by a crescent of tropical trees.

A ripple of sound fell through the air, a slight motion, like the wind from an unfurled blanket of rust red. Far in the east, hot blood touched the cold, paper sky.

He walked up the beach and entered the resin scented jungle. The trees were tall and thin, smooth and waxy like celery, crisp, yet a rich, emerald green. Great triangle leaves like vast arrows sprouted from their base, shooting several metres high to form pointed darts. George leaned back to look at the tops of these great plants to see huge flower heads looming down over him, massive yellow hands with trumpet mouths; daffodils, with a family of shivering stamens inside their bells, pointing down at George like golden fire pokers. He looked around to find himself in a forest of these flowers which seemed to surround the lake from which he had just emerged, the blooms gazing down into its mirror surface, mesmerised, yet forlorn.

George placed his hand onto the great stem of the flower nearby and the head lit up brightly like a street lamp.

Far away, far in the upper air, where the tiny spirits ran and played, far in the warm currents of love and lugubrious ozone, far in that sea of lost particle beings and the cool fingers of stars' breath, there was a movement; a faint whisper of the sound of a bell on the breeze, an echo choke that smelled of copper and tin.

In a crackle, the daffodil instantly changed into a street lamp, a shaft of zinc steel, reaching up to a glowing head. In a blast, the night exploded into bright day and the fern curls of the forest exploded into the jagged concrete of a steel city. Every flower became a street light, every plant a person, a litter bin, a bicycle. George found himself standing on a pavement beside a road of noise, commotion, screaming motorcycles, beeping cars, choking smoke and swarming people; people, moving, pushing, bumping along like salmon.

THE CITY

The grey claws of the city raked the floor with their cement smell. The air hummed with the infinite buzz of emotional energy, the electric pulse of a billion excited hearts; people walking and talking on telephones, sitting and smoking, wearing sunglasses like fifties film stars, friends drinking coffee, women stumbling with armfuls of bags, dragging children on chains, dogs on strings, cats in arms. Wide cars swam along their tarmac rivers, belching out their oily breaths, while daredevil cyclists flew between their whale-hulks. Everywhere energy and movement.

It was morning, and somewhat chilly. The mirrored windows clasped at an orange glow, the happy smile of new beginnings.

George stood there, motionless, a statue in this new maze. His mind was deep down, deep away inside near some wintered core. Deep down there, his hands were stroking the ice of his heart, brushing off the water.

A silver flying robot, about the size of a kestrel, buzzed up to George like an inquisitive fly, pulling him into lucidity. Its body was a glass cube, a glowing red light that pulsated on and off in irregular excited skips. The robot ejected a steely tentacle towards George as though it were a butterfly tasting the air for nectar. It emitted a gaggle of beeps and electronic sounds: 'Tagga tagga. Tak tak tak tak. Tagga tagga.'

The machine seemed to be happy. It flew away on

whirling blades, buzzing along the street to probe another sleepy denizen.

The tip of George's heart began to sun-glow, dipped into liquid bronze, like the steely corners of the buildings. Around his island body, the incessant river of people flowed, fast and slow. In front of him was a light glass door that led in to a shopping arcade. A steady stream of shoppers headed in and out of the crystal palace like eager bees.

She was in there, waiting for him. He had always known it. It was a strange realisation, that in the great machine palace of his mind, the obvious realities were the ones he most ignored. He often focused on the difficult parts, the uncertain parts, when the obvious things were completely bypassed. He could easily, for example, walk, or move an arm without even thinking how or why; he just did it. Did it, and there it was. There was no question of how, or of any difficulties. It suddenly seemed quite amazing just how obvious it was that Lucine was in the shopping centre waiting for him right now, and always had been. Why didn't he even notice it before?!

An electric ripple of excitement ran through him, delighting his body into action. He dashed towards the glass panel door and slid it open with perfect smoothness.

The shopping arcade was like a wide corridor, skinned with coffee coloured marble. The ceiling was an arch of glass, clasping the dome air with a spider of white ribs to separate it from the azure sky beyond. Shoppers flowed like fish along the polished pathway, flowing in and out of the shops that lined each side. Groups stared lustfully into the crystal windows and their fantasy contents. Tinny dance music was playing from a distant electric mouth; thud thud thud.

George stood on tiptoes to see if he could see Lucine somewhere among the crowds. He couldn't see her.

'Hey!' A voice called above the hubbub: 'Hey, George!'

It was Crevel. He was a few meters away, separated by a flow of human traffic. He held on to his trilby hat and slid through the crowd, twisting, apologising. Eventually he reached George: 'Wow it's busy in here isn't it!?' he said.

'Look at this, look what I've just bought!' He pulled back his sleeve to show George a sparkly gold watch. The time showed eleven o'clock. 'A beauty isn't it?' he beamed.

'Oh that's nice,' said George, disinterested, but polite.

'I have a wife now too,' said an excited Crevel. 'Look, there.' Crevel pointed across the arcade to a distant woman wearing a black ball-gown of ruffled satin. Her face was turned away, her eyes peering into the blazing window of a jeweller's shop. A cascade of blonde hair flowed down her back. She looked like Lucine. Next to her, equally enraptured by the glittering window, was a small boy with black hair. His little face was close to the glass, his tiny pink fingers touching its thick warmness to impress it with the grey vapours of breath and finger oil. The boy looked like a young George, the glowing child; but this boy's ears, could they be a little bit pointed?

'Darling!' Crevel waved at the distant woman like a lost sailor. She didn't hear him above the hum, the crude jangling music. George looked towards the woman in hope and longing. Was it her, at last? After a few seconds she casually turned to glance at them both, and she caught George's gaze. He was embarrassed to see that it wasn't Lucine. Her face was very similar to Lucine's, but this face was older, and wearing too much make-up. She seemed somehow false, as though she were trying to emulate Lucine. Her black dress; it looked exactly like the one in Crevel's old photograph, the one Lucine had been wearing, but surely, this wasn't it either. It was an imitation.

A brutish man suddenly bumped between George and Crevel; a short lump of a man with a black beard and a tan coat that draped over his mound of a back, and dragged, hissing over the tiles behind him. The man grunted a crude apology and shambled towards the crystal exit doors, pausing before them and ripping off a bite of black bread from his hairy clutches before leaving.

Something caught George's eye, someone moving amidst the swarm of shoppers. It was Neiro, a small bounding little imp, snaking between the legs of the crowd. Neiro paused, and turned to wave at George with his encouraging smile, his little face lit by the orange glow of dawn. George made a quick apology to Crevel and quickly stepped on, squeezing through the crowd along the arcade towards Neiro, his tiny body darting in and out of sight up ahead.

George, the leaf in the brook, floating in the sunlit water.

In the centre of the arcade was a clock, a brass faced mock-relic mounted on a cube of pink stone. It was suspended from the ceiling on bronzed arches that curled and flowed, carved with acanthus leaves and waves. Its short hand groaned, then clicked the passing hour with a loud chime, sending a single metal cry around this hollow glass palace. The music began to play a song about a sandman.

George had lost Neiro and was in sight of the exit doors at the end of the arcade, a glass wall that led to a concrete field of nothingness. He desperately looked around for the little imp, his little friend.

Hunched by the exit door was a hill of a man wearing heavy rags, his hunched bones bent under thick brown-green sacks. His face was draped in the shadows from the twisted flop of a hat made of dirty tweed. His left hand was gloved, and gripped a black dog lead attached to a grey skinned dog; an ugly lump of a beast with wide yellow eyes. Little shivering feather wings sprouted from its silvery back. It was Neiro.

The man raised his cowering head to reveal a unshaven face of pock-marked redded skin. His eyes were black, jet dark, and made of liquid malevolence. His mouth slowly formed into a wicked grin and he raised his right hand from his coat. It held a dagger with a blade of infinite blackness that radiated an anti-light of darkness and coldness, the knife won by the savage ape. In one swift motion, the man drew back his arm and threw the blade at George. It flew through the air in a laser line, drawing a black thread streak, a streak of cold death, a beam of midnight with the scream of dawn, the scream of a thousand black birds exploding.

Then from the crowd between the man and George, a woman stepped out, a woman with a tumble of straw gold hair and wearing a long white dress that flowed like a sunfall. She stepped right into the dagger's path and it flew into her, hitting her like a steel mallet wrapped in leather pushing into a band of bell-bronze. The perfect white ripples of her dress waved like a tumbling ocean of stars, opened like a liquid cream clam shell, then closed in on the dark blade, swallowing it like a vast and white sun engulfing a dead moon.

He always knew she would come.

George and Lucine were instantly outside in the vast plain of winter's dawn, standing together as one in front of the great dark door.

A gold crescent sliced the frost sky of night blue, drawing a thin line of copper blood from east to west.

The sky of pink-iron crackled into lightening day over them. The zags and zigs of crystal night melted into soft tears as winter retreated her soft fingers, sliding them back towards the closing doorway, back and away, leaving the couple together again in the arms of soft summer.

It was over; and ready to begin.

LIGHT

Bird of fire, cast as a thread
of copper adamant in heavy ocean's air,
calm me with your warm bed
of destiny and glass prayer.

We fates sew the sky with light,
a line of beacons to guide the way,
and comfort coldness in uncertain night
with laser truth to seize the day.

Come, Ozymandias! Reach your great arm
to heaven's dome and roar,
stride the desert sea, in raging calm
and nuclear hate-love awe.

Gaze, king of kings, at your infinite field of black white.
Prove your mastery; rise, fly,
loosen every dream from night's dark chains
and cast them screaming into the bright sky.

Other written works by Mark Sheeky

as Author

365 Universes, Pentangel Books (2012)
The Many Beautiful Worlds of Death, Pentangel Books (2015)
21st Century Surrealism, Pentangel Books (2018)

as Illustrator

Songs Of Life, Pentangel Books (2014)
Testing the Delicates, Ink Pantry Publishing (2017)
Songs of Innocence and of Experience, Pentangel Books (2018)

as Contributor

Hide It!, Mardibooks (2014)
The Ball of the Future, Earlyworks Press (2015)
Journeys Beyond, Earlyworks Press (2015)
Diversifly, Fair Acre Press (2018)

www.marksheeky.com

Printed in Great Britain
by Amazon